S0-AWH-729

The Soul of the Silver Dog

Other books by Lynn Hall

The Tormentors

Murder in a Pig's Eye

In Trouble Again, *Zelda Hammersmith?*

Zelda Strikes Again!

Here Comes Zelda Claus
and Other Holiday Disasters

Murder at the Spaniel Show

The Secret Life of Dagmar Schultz

Flyaway

The Solitary

If Winter Comes

Mrs. Portree's Pony

The Giver

The Soul of the Silver Dog

Lynn Hall

Harcourt Brace Jovanovich, Publishers
San Diego New York London

Library of Congress Cataloging-in-Publication Data
Hall, Lynn.
The soul of the silver dog/by Lynn Hall.
p. cm.
Summary: Feeling rejected by her own family after her younger sister's death, fourteen-year-old Cory adopts a blind show dog and devotes herself to bringing back some of his championship glory by training him for agility competition.
ISBN 0-15-277196-4
[1. Dogs—Fiction. 2. Dog shows—Fiction.] I. Title.
PZ7.H1458Sp 1991
[Fic]—dc20 91-11072

Printed in the United States of America

First edition
Designed by Lydia D'moch
A B C D E

The Soul of the Silver Dog

The dog braced his legs and stood rigid against the slow roll of the planet beneath him. A chill wind pushed against him, threatening his balance.

He knew he was in the dog yard. He recognized the gravel under his feet and the smell of the borzois' urine on the fence. The angle of the sun against his skin gave him a sense of midday.

The ache of his bladder urged him to move. He took a tottering step, then another, then squatted. The acrid wetness that splashed against his front legs and chest bothered him, but he was afraid to lift his leg, afraid of losing his balance.

He moved ahead a few steps in a cautious half squat, until a branch struck his face. Whining softly, he lowered his head to rub his eye against his foreleg. First one eye, then the other, he pressed against his leg and rubbed. He blinked and lifted his head toward the sun's warmth.

Where there should have been glaring light in his eyes there was nothing.

He heard voices; crunching footsteps on gravel. Cautiously, fearful for his balance, he turned his long, lean head toward the sounds. His tail trembled against his hocks.

The woman's voice and the girl's were familiar, well learned in the weeks since he'd been here. But there was a third voice this morning. He cocked his head and listened. Another girl's voice, softer and deeper pitched, and sounding less often than the other two voices.

He heard the rustling of clothing, felt the warmth of approaching bodies. He extended his head and felt a hand under his jaw forming a trough, a support. The hand remained steady as he shifted his body toward the girl with the soft voice. He leaned more deeply into the hand.

Within the aura of the girl's warmth, supported by her strength, he ceased to be aware of the movement of the planet beneath his legs. For an instant he absorbed the girl's essence and something of his soul blended with her.

He closed his useless eyes and sagged against her.

One

Corianne wept. It was silent and swift and contained, but when she touched the dog and felt him lean against her hand, she was overcome.

When Lee had called this morning to tell her about the dog, Corianne had come reluctantly. There had been too much compassion forced from her already. She didn't want to have to look at a blind dog. She might have glanced at this one and turned away but for the tremulous wagging of his tail against his hock and the way his head had turned toward her voice.

Now she sat on the gravel and eased the dog's body against hers, still holding his head in her palm. Through her jacket she felt his tension. She stroked him, smoothing him with her hand until his trembling eased.

He was a Bedlington terrier, built like a small greyhound wrapped in a coat of silver cotton. Corianne had seen him a few times since he'd come from the show kennel in California, but she hadn't touched him until now and she was startled by the softness of his inch-long coat. He was like a plush toy.

No, not a toy. Within that elegant head were pain and confusion and fear. Although his body was relaxed now against hers, his head remained in tense, heavy contact with her hand. She dared not take her hand away, until at last he moved his head himself, to rub his eye against her chest.

"What are you going to do with him?" she asked Lee's mother, who stood with Lee behind her.

"Sue the bastard who sold him to me, for starters," Trish Winterbottom said in her executive voice. "Three thousand dollars we paid for that dog. So he's a group winner and an international champion, big deal. He's not worth diddly to us now, and that breeder knew damned well he had canine glaucoma when she sold him to us. The vet said he'd have to have been showing symptoms for quite a while. No way they didn't know they were selling us a blind dog."

In her soft, husky voice Corianne said, "Yes, but what are you going to do with him? With Sterling?"

The woman shrugged. "Put him down, I suppose. Unless you want him. You want him?" It was an off-hand question; already the woman was moving toward the house, clutching her shaggy fun-fur jacket around her chin. She barely heard Corianne's breathy "Yes."

The Winterbottom house was one of Galena's tour homes. The small northwest Illinois town was given over almost entirely to tourism and antiques and quaint summer homes for Chicagoans. General Grant's home was a major visitor attraction, along with the ski resorts, the rugged limestone semi-mountains, and the lead mines. Old brick and stone homes of historic or architectural interest were opened to the public twice a year on home-tour weekends, when busloads of visitors went from house to house looking and taking pictures. Corianne's mother worked seasonally as a tour guide.

Winterbottom House was close to the center of town and had started life as a winery. It was a square brick building, flat-topped, its boxiness softened by rounded windows and doors, by forests of ivy and delicate wrought-iron trim. Carousel horses flanked the black double doors. A head-high brick wall extended from the building to enclose the back lawn, which was a combination of formal garden and exercise area for the Winterbottoms' show dogs—an elderly saluki, a whippet, and a pair of magnificent borzois.

Corianne had been coming to this house all her life; otherwise she'd have been intimidated by its grandeur. Cory and Lee had ridden the carousel horses in a tandem gallop through their childhoods. Lee had been "Lisa" then.

As cute little girls and later as unlovely elongated children they had shared ski lessons at Chestnut Mountain, flailing their ways down the bunny slopes. They had slept curled together on the dinette bed in the Winterbottoms' motor home on dog-show weekends, and had held fast to each other through family storms.

At fourteen they were known to their friends as Cory-and-Lee, a single entity, not to be invited anywhere separately. Their other friendships were shallow and changeable and not very important to either of them.

Lee sat now on the frosty gravel beside Cory and stroked the dog. Her features were maturing along lines of classic beauty, but she did everything she could to undermine it. Her hair was an inch long; she never wore makeup or clothes more flattering than jeans and T-shirts, although her closet made Cory whimper sometimes in sheer envy. She had begun calling herself Lee and refused to answer to Lisa.

"Are you really going to keep Sterling?" she asked.

"Yes." Cory bit the word off decisively.

"Will your mom let you?"

"I think so, now that Bethy is . . ."

But she couldn't quite say "now that Bethy is dead," so she let the sentence fade.

It occurred to her that there might be a connection between this dog's going blind and her nightly begging to God for her sister to die. Crime and punishment. She longed for logic, but logic would have meant blindness for herself, not for an innocent dog whom she hadn't even known when his blindness started. No. She was safe. She hadn't caused the dog's suffering.

In the house a telephone rang.

"What are you going to do with a blind dog?" Lee asked curiously.

Cory thought about it. "I'm going to give him a happy life."

If I can do that, she thought, maybe it will partway make up for Bethy.

Trish Winterbottom emerged from the house at her usual energetic pace, designer slacks flashing below the fun-fur jacket, car keys swinging from her finger. "Have to go meet a client. If Daddy calls, tell him I'm out at the Lusk listing with the Gundersons and I should be back by lunchtime unless they decide to make an offer, in which case I'll be at the office and he can catch me there. If I don't get back, there's some lasagna left; just warm it in the mike—and Cory, you stay if you want or I can run you home. If you're going to take the dog now, you won't be able to manage him on your bike. If you girls want to ski I can drive you out later this afternoon, but I don't think the snow's going to be much good, this warm. Got to go. Cory?"

"I'll walk, thanks. Is it all right? Can I go ahead and take him home with me?"

"Sure. I was going to have the vet put him down tomorrow. You might as well take him if you want him and if your mother says it's okay. Three thousand dollars down the toilet." She slammed herself into her compact Cadillac.

Lee looked at Cory and said, "How are you going to get him home? I don't think he'll walk on a lead." She stood up, but when Cory moved to follow, the dog pressed himself hard against her. Gently she set him on his legs and knelt beside him, her hand still against his throat, steadying him.

Lee ran to the house and came back with one of the narrow nylon show leads from the kennel room. Corianne slipped its noose end over Sterling's head and settled it where a show dog wears his lead, just behind his ears. She stood up then and urged him forward with a gentle tug.

He stiffened, and his sightless eyes grew wide with fear.

"I'll carry him," Corianne said. "I'll come back for my bike."

"You want me to come with?"

"No. I don't know what Mom's going to say. I better do it alone."

"Right. You want to go ski this aft?"

Cory shook her head. "I'll have to take care of him." She bent and eased the dog into her arms, and carried him lamb fashion, his legs dangling. He twisted his neck until his head was pressed against her shoulder.

Four downhill blocks she carried him, toward the bridge at the core of the town. It was a handsome bridge over the Galena River, built of brick and mounted with ornate lampposts, but today Corianne didn't notice. Her arms ached with the weight of the dog. She stopped from time to time to shift him or to rest him against her upraised knee.

Ten o'clock on a March Sunday morning. Church bells played a carillon tune, marred by the opposing clanging from a steeple across the valley.

Two blocks beyond the bridge, where the land began its climb against limestone bluffs, Corianne's boots turned up a serpentine brick path to a storybook cottage. This house was included in the historic-homes tours also, but it was at the opposite extreme from the Winterbottom House. This was a dollhouse, a miniature delight built of crude handmade brick and sagging timbers. It was set far back from the street on a tree-dotted lawn, against the base of a sheer limestone bluff that rose two hundred feet above it.

The little house was charming, with its small, low-ceilinged rooms, fireplaces tucked into corners, and foot-hollowed steps up and down from room to room. It was dark always, shaded by its trees and the bluff, and the air carried a faint, rocky dampness.

Charming it was, but a cramped prison for Cory when four of them had lived here—her father and her mother and herself, and Bethy. Bethy's hospital-type bed had taken up most of the tiny dining room, and all of life had centered on it. Now, with only Cory and her mother left here, the little house was taking a deep breath and expanding. The dining room was a dining room again, and the French doors could once again be opened onto the back garden. With Bethy there, the damp outdoor air had been too great a risk.

The house was silent. Cory listened for her mother, sensed that she was still upstairs in bed. She set the dog down long enough to take off her jacket, then picked him up again and sat with him on a cushioned footstool beside the fireplace. There were live embers in the ash bed from last night's fire; Cory was able to twist far enough to put another piece of wood into the fireplace without leaving the dog. Then she held him lightly against her side and waited.

The room was small and square and dark, its windows half blocked by shrubs. Rug and furniture were dark, rich shades of blue and red; the fireplace wall was of dark brick and darker timbers. The white walls might have brightened the little room, but they were too thickly covered with watercolor paintings of Galena scenes, with antique horse brasses and bed warmers. It was a room to look at, not to live in.

Corianne and Sterling sat motionless, waiting, until at last the upstairs floors creaked, water ran, and the toilet flushed, and finally Nan Wendel groped down the steep, narrow stairway. She wore bunny slippers and a quilted robe, and her hair went in all directions at once.

It was soft, dark hair against an English-rose complexion. She had been beautiful before her face and body had begun expanding, but she hadn't been aware of her beauty. Her husband had never mentioned it to her.

She stopped in the doorway, startled. "Good Lord, what's that, a sheep? What are you doing with it?"

Cory's elbow tensed against Sterling and drew him tighter against her side. "He's not a sheep, he's a Bedlington terrier. This is the one Lee's folks just bought from California for three thousand dollars. I told you. He went blind. Lee said their vet said he has glaucoma. Her mom was going to have him put down, but she said I could have him if I wanted him."

Nan grunted, squinted her face against decisions, and shuffled into the kitchen. She started the coffee, then shuffled back, her eyes open a degree wider although the coffee was still only a fragrance.

"Blind, huh?"

Corianne nodded and said, "Yes, but dogs can get along really well without their sight, lots better than people can. They depend on their other senses a lot more than we do, and a blind dog can get around just fine in a familiar place. I really want him, Mom. I really need to have this dog."

Nan closed one eye and stared thoughtfully at Cory with the other. "Are you sure you want to take on that kind of responsibility? You've lived in this family long enough to know what it can mean, taking care of somebody who can't take care of himself."

Choosing her words carefully, Cory said, "Yes, but you wanted Bethy. You loved Bethy a lot more than . . . a lot more than you would have if she'd been normal. Don't you think I'm as good a person as you are?"

Nan's hands flew into the air. "It's not the same thing. Bethy was ours. She was our child. We had no choice in the matter. You're taking on a job you don't have to take on, honey. I'm not saying you shouldn't do it, I just want to be sure you know what you'd be letting yourself in for."

"I don't care about that," Cory said. And she didn't care. This dog, this warm body pressed against hers, was more than something to be possessed. He was hers in a profound and complex way; his essence, his need were seeping into the hollows of her heart.

The coffee maker signaled, and Nan rose. "I don't care, then. But the work is all yours, hear? And keep him off that good carpet in there."

An unexpected flood of tears coursed down Cory's face. She had never cried easily. But now she dropped her face to the silvery wool and wrapped both arms hard around the dog. He twisted to lick at the tears.

"It's okay," she murmured. "You're going to live here with me and have a wonderful life, and we're going to love each other so much that we won't need anybody else ever, ever. I'll teach you everything, and help you, and love you."

The dog whined softly and smacked his tail against the cushion.

Sterling's dream was vividly colored and sharply focused, as if his brain were trying to compensate for vision denied.

The scenes rushed past him, flashes of white crisscross show-ring fencing, the rear end of a dog in front of him as they charged around the ring, the face of a judge looming close to his own as she peered at his teeth. These were the scenes he remembered most clearly from his sighted life. The pale plastic walls of his crate had bounded his world outside the show ring. There had been twice-daily whirls around an exercise run, and long hours standing on the grooming table in the kennel while his sensitive ears and throat and tail were shaved with electric clippers and the rest of his coat was slowly carved with snipping shears. But all of his life outside the show ring had been mere preparation and waiting.

Only in the ring, with his handler's tension igniting his own, had he been fully alive. Those scenes now were the ones that his curtained eyes saw as he slept. His eyelids trembled, his paws twitched as he moved in his fast prancing trot around the ring for the final sweep that ended in his handler's whoop of joy, his own leap into the air in response. Over his head ribbons and trophies were handed, congratulations given; but for him the apex of the excitement was the circling of the ring with joy fizzing through him, and the leap at the end.

He began rising through sleep toward consciousness, aware now that he was in a strange place. Beneath him was an expanse of warmth and softness, and against his spine was the comforting mass of his mother. He was a tiny puppy stretched out against the creature who was the source of his life.

No. The fog of sleep cleared from his brain and he knew it was not his mother against whom he slept, but the girl with the husky voice. The girl. She had cradled his head yesterday and made the planet hold still for him to balance on it.

The girl.

There is an instinct in dogs that makes Border collies crouch and herd, that makes beagles hone in on rabbit scent and Newfoundlands pull swimmers from the water. It is a joyful recognition of purpose.

Sterling felt a stirring in the deepest part of him as he lay against the girl. It was a recognition of purpose. The girl. The girl was his purpose. . . .

Two

Corianne stirred from her dreams and rolled onto her side to rest her hand on the silver dog, to stare at him with unfocused awe. Careful not to wake him, she snagged her glasses from the bookcase headboard of her bed so she could study him more clearly.

On the close-shaved ears and cheeks his skin was silvery blue. On the ends of his ears were puffed tassels of white cotton to match the curly topknot on his head. As she watched, his eyelids ceased their twitching and began to crack, showing a sliver of black eyeball within.

So much to do, she thought. Talk to the vet and find out if he needs any medicine for his eyes. Find out how much it will cost to buy the combs and scissors and clippers to keep him beautiful.

Last night Lee's mother had driven over, bringing Cory's bike and Sterling's fiberglass crate. Cory had wanted him to have a safe, familiar place to be in when she couldn't be with him. The crate was beside her bed now.

He woke and rolled toward her onto his back, head twisted to one side, forelegs folded coyly under his chin. As her hand stroked his chest, his tail thrashed.

Cory got up finally and made a fast run to the bathroom, then pulled on sweatshirt and pants and woolly boots. Sterling lay on his belly now, feeling his way toward the edge of the bed, panting uneasily and listening for her.

"Wait a minute. I'll carry you."

She scooped him up and carried him downstairs and out through the French doors into the bluff garden, grabbing her jacket as she went. She set him carefully on his feet and slipped the show lead over his head.

"It's okay. You can walk. Flat ground all around." She took a step and waited while he found the courage to follow. The next step was easier, and in a few minutes he was walking almost normally at her side.

The bluff garden was the space between the back of the house and the wall of creamy limestone, the base of the soaring bluffs. Limestone rocks were fitted together to make thick walls, waist high, on either end of the little garden, walls set with dark green plank gates. The garden itself was threaded with curved paths of herringboned brick and rimmed with flower borders, dead now in late winter.

Corianne and Sterling had spent much of yesterday afternoon in this garden, walking in slow circles while

Sterling sniffed the ground, the brick paths, the dead stalks of snapdragon and columbine. Now he remembered. He remembered its pattern, its boundaries.

Suddenly joyful, he leaped as he'd leaped in the show ring, and pulled against the lead. Laughing, Cory ran with him. Then she knelt and slipped off the lead.

Sterling froze. Nothing was touching him, nothing supporting him. The girl was there, but too far away. . . . He braced his legs as the earth began its slow, upsetting motion beneath him.

"Want it back on?" She replaced the lead and stroked his throat, steadying him. "It's okay, I'm right here. I'll go with you. Come on, we can run a little bit, stretch your legs. That's it, that's it. Yay, Sterling!"

Their first week together passed with growing ease and pleasure for Corianne and Sterling. They romped in the bluff garden at dawn, he slept curled in the safe familiarity of his crate while she was at school, and in the evenings they were inseparable. They took longer walks every day, then settled down for homework or TV or reading, with Sterling stretched contentedly beside the girl, his head across her foot.

Their afternoon walks began in the bluff garden. The long, tree-dotted front yard was their next training ground, then, as Sterling's confidence grew, the sidewalks of Bluff Street. It was a quiet street that curved along the base of the bluff, with little traffic to frighten Sterling. Most of the houses were antique make-overs, like Cory's, and many were owned by city people who used them only on weekends, so the neighborhood was Cory's and Sterling's on those raw March afternoons.

As a show dog, Sterling had gaited on a tight lead, always at his handler's left side, keeping pace or moving slightly ahead, always against the lead, which rode high on his neck just behind his ears. He walked that way now with Cory, keeping the warm aura of her body and her scents just to the right of his head, the lead taut between them.

Cory learned to handle the lead like the snaffle rein on a finely trained show horse. Keeping it gently taut, she could signal with the merest pressure when an obstacle appeared.

"Down," she'd say, or "Up," and slow him with the lead. Within a few days he understood the two words and stepped accordingly, up or down a curb or step. Not realizing she was doing it, Cory shortened or lengthened the words according to the size of the step, and Sterling learned these subtleties, too.

Cory's mother stopped at the vet's on her way home from work on Thursday and picked up a dropper bottle of medication for Sterling's eyes. Two drops in each eye morning and night, to relieve the pressure within the diseased eyeballs. Cory paid the bill, twelve dollars, from the last of her birthday money.

By the second week, Sterling's coat was beginning to form matted balls above his feet and inside his elbows, and the clean lines of his head were blurred beneath the growing coat. His skin no longer showed blue on his ears and throat. He needed grooming.

Sterling's confidence on the lead had improved so much by the middle of that week that Cory walked him, on Thursday afternoon, toward downtown and the Kanine Klip Joint. It was in a shoddy, narrow building on a shoddy, narrow street just off the main business area of town. Cory pushed open the door, told Sterling "Up . . . up . . . ," and went in.

It was a small, square room with linoleum floors and tan-painted walls and counters. Racks of leashes and grooming tools and squeaky toys lined the walls. No one was in sight, but rock music came from a back room, and a hoarse voice sang along. Cory rang the bell on the counter.

"Hold on, be right with you," the voice bellowed.

The woman who eventually emerged was smaller than the voice had promised, a hard-faced, wiry woman with unbelievably black hair, and a cigarette bobbing in her mouth.

"Hey, a Bedlington. I ain't done a Bedlington since I left Florida. Lots of 'em down there. Don't see 'em around the Midwest much. What can I do you out of?"

She wore a huge grooming apron with a picture of two dogs tearing each other apart and the words Don't Mess with Me, I'm the Biggest Bitch in the Kennel.

"I was wondering if you could help me," Cory said apologetically. "I just got this dog and I don't have any money to pay for getting him groomed, but I want to keep him looking nice and I want to do it myself. I was wondering if you maybe knew where I could get some used clippers cheap, or something like that. . . ."

"Huh. Not going to be a paying customer, huh?"

"I'm not old enough to get a job," Cory pleaded, "but I really love him, and I want . . ."

"Don't get your toes in an uproar, I was just putting you on. Hell, I got more customers than I can handle as it is, and scissor-finishing a Bedlington—honey, that's work. Used clippers, huh? In your dreams. Nobody hardly ever gets rid of used clippers. New ones, now, I can lend you a catalog where you could order clippers, they'd be about seventy bucks, and you'd need a good Belgian greyhound comb for that coat, another fifteen, twenty bucks, and your shears, you don't want to spend anything less than about fifty bucks on your shears or they won't hold an edge and you'll have to be sending them off all the time to get them sharpened."

Cory wilted. Sterling's food and medication were going to take every penny of her allowances and gift money. Babysitting . . . maybe. She'd never done it and dreaded having to. Small children scared her, the responsibility of them and the way they stared at her. And it would take forever to earn enough for all this grooming stuff, especially in a town where so many families came only on weekends and had no children.

The groomer came around the counter and reached down abruptly toward Sterling. The dog cringed.

"Kinda timid, is he?"

"He's not timid. He's blind. He has glaucoma and he's only been blind for a couple of weeks, so he's not used to things yet. That's how come his owner gave him to me. He's a group-winning champion from California and they paid three thousand dollars for him."

The groomer whistled softly through her teeth and approached Sterling again more gently. He accepted her touch and whipped his tail.

"I thought he looked like a good one. That's a gorgeous head on him. A mile long, ain't it. Yeah, you can see he's got breeding. That's a shame about the glaucoma, but at least it looks like he's landed in a pot of honey with you. Yeah, see here on his brisket, his coat's matting up already. These soft, nonshedding coats, you really have to stay on top of them or they'll mat up on you overnight. Everybody wants dogs that don't shed, like the poodles and Bedlingtons, but then they don't know enough to keep the dead hair combed out, and they end up with matted messes."

The woman scooped Sterling into her arms and bore him into the back room. "Come on back here, I'll show you what to do. What's your name, anyway? I'm Iva. Here, we'll just set him on this table over here, and you can work on him while I finish up this bastard I was working on."

Cory looked at the dog on the other grooming table. He was a caramel-colored cocker spaniel, half shaved and half covered with fist-sized balls of matted hair. He glared at Cory over the strip of cloth that bound his mouth shut.

"That's Augie," Iva said. "Cocker from Hell, we call him around here. He generally nails me two or three times before I get the muzzle on him." She held out her arm and showed Cory the pair of tooth holes on her wrist, already scabbing over.

The two of them glared at each other, cocker and groomer, each with a lifted lip and a low snarl.

"Here you go," Iva said, turning back to Cory. "Slip his head into the grooming noose there; that'll keep him steady and comfortable. Here's your Belgian greyhound comb; start at the feet and work up, a little bit at a time; go all the way down to the skin and pull out the dead coat and all the little bits of mats starting to form. When you get up to those big mats behind his legs, bite in at the outer edges with the teeth — see, like this — and work the dead stuff out. When you get him all combed out, I'll show you how to work the clippers, and you can take him down on his head and ears."

She returned to the cocker, snarled at him, and picked up her clippers.

For the next hour Cory worked over Sterling in absolute happiness. She sang along with the radio and Iva, and listened to the woman's gravelly voice shouting advice over the music and the buzz of the clippers.

The Cocker from Hell was duly denuded, bathed, and dried, and emerged wagging happily and kissing

Iva, who stuffed a dog treat into the mouth she'd muzzled earlier. When his owner came to pick him up Augie pranced away wearing a tiny neckerchief and looking as though he had won the battle.

Iva pocketed the twenty-dollar grooming fee and the twenty-dollar nasty-dog tip that his apologetic owner always paid, and smiled at her own victory.

Cory set the newly trimmed Sterling on the floor and asked, "How much do I owe you for using your stuff?"

"Nah." Iva waved her away. "Listen, this is a special dog you got here, kid. You come and use my stuff whenever you want. Hey, you could give me a hand sometimes if you want, on a Saturday. I get busier than a cranberry merchant on Saturdays; I could use a bather. Anytime you want to come by and help, come ahead. I'll trade you even-Steven. Groom your own dog with my equipment—trade off for a morning's worth of helping me. We both win, and it won't cost either of us anything."

Cory's eyes lit. "I'd love to. But not this weekend, okay? I'm going to some dog shows with my girlfriend, but if you really need me I could . . ."

"Nah, whenever you got time."

"Thanks again," Cory breathed and held the door open for Sterling. "Sterling, down . . . down . . ."

They walked home with Cory doing dance steps to the music that echoed in her head from Iva's radio. Sterling pranced and leaped against her.

Sterling felt an overflowing joy. The hour spent standing on the grooming table had given him a comfortable sense of rightness. The pull and bite of the comb, the noise and buzz and scrape of the clippers against his throat, all of it was familiar. It reassured him that he was still himself despite the curtains in his eyes.

It had been weeks now since he had run on his own. He longed to stretch and flex his body in a race against his shadow, to feel the pull of his leg muscles and the grip of his feet against the earth, to gouge his nails into the dirt and make it fly up behind him as he ran.

He leaped up toward the girl to show his joy and lunged into the lead. If she would run beside him to keep him safe, he could do it. He plunged against the lead, begging her.

"What? You want to run? Okay, let's go."

It was glorious!

Then it was over, and the brick path was beneath his pads again, and the smell of the damp rocks.

"Up . . . up," she told him, and he knew they were at the front steps of home.

Inside the house he stopped and tensed. A man's voice came from the kitchen. When the girl bent to slip off his lead her fingers moved stiffly against his skin, and her voice grew strained.

He didn't follow her toward the man. Uneasy, he wanted the security of his crate. He could move through the house safely by now because the girl had led him around each room countless times, showing him with her hand where objects stood. She'd led him up to chairs and walls and tapped the things so that he could hear where they were, could sniff them and memorize them.

The girl turned away from him now and went toward the man's voice, leaving Sterling on his own. He trotted across the open space that lay between him and the stairs, concentrating on getting himself to his crate.

Suddenly something cracked him in the face.

He yipped and froze. His old terror washed through him, and he braced against the movement of the planet.

Three

"You moved the chair," Cory said furiously. She held Sterling against her, stroked him, and glared across his trembling body at the man who stood in the kitchen doorway.

Ron Wendel was a rather small man, with a close and expensive haircut and slim mustache, and clothes tailored to his narrow body. *Dapper* seemed to be his target. Since changing wives he'd begun wearing a snug gold chain at the base of his neck, like a dog's collar. Corianne thought it looked ridiculous, but then everything about him set her teeth on edge now.

"Sorry," he said blandly. "I moved the chair a few inches. I needed to get into the magazine rack. I don't believe that calls for temper tantrums."

"My dog is blind!" Cory said. "I told you, and Mom told you. If you move things he hurts himself on them. Mom and I are careful about it. I should think you could remember it when you come to visit."

Bitterness tainted the last words. She felt the dog begin to tremble again. She picked him up and carried him up the narrow stairway toward the haven of her room.

"Apologize to your father," Nan called, but with little force. Cory pretended not to hear.

Tenderly she placed Sterling on the bed and got his bottle of eye drops from the headboard. He crept up to the pillows and sprawled there, finally able to relax. It wasn't time for his drops yet, but Cory needed to do something for him.

He submitted to her thumb against his lids, the cool splash of the medication against his eyeballs. He'd already begun to understand that after the drops came an easing of the pressure inside his eyes.

Cory got her history book and crawled onto the bed beside Sterling in her sitting-up position for reading. There was a chapter on the Boer War to read before tomorrow, but she couldn't even open the book when there was so much going on inside her. Sterling wiggled up against her until his body lay across her chest, his head pressed against her neck. As she rubbed his stomach his black lips stretched into his form of smile and his long, slim tail beat against the bed.

Bending over the bed just then, putting the medication into Sterling's eyes, Cory had had a flash of recognition that had added to the emotional storm her father had roused. Just for that instant, bending over Sterling, she had become her mother bending over Bethy.

Her eyes dampened. She took off her glasses and leaned her head back against the pillow and stroked Sterling with slow, hypnotic movements. The tension was eased, stroke by stroke, but the old sad ache remained.

They'd been a happy little family once, a storybook family living in this little storybook house. Cory's memories of that time were clear and detailed. She had been her parents' little girl, walking between them, swinging from their arms. They'd be walking three abreast, down the sidewalk or through the zoo, and without warning Cory would pick up her feet and drop her weight onto their arms, and they always caught her. They'd laugh and swing her between them until she kicked free and regained her own footing.

They did things for her then. They took her on riverboat rides in Dubuque, on the huge paddle wheeler that served fancy dinners and had funny plays on its stage. They took her to the zoo almost as often as she wanted to go, and for her birthday they gave her a kitten of her own. When she was sick they stayed home from work to play games with her.

But then there was the summer when she was eight, and Mom's tummy got round and huge. They both explained to Cory about the new baby brother or sister, and they pressed her palm against the place where the baby was growing, so she could feel it kicking.

She'd been mildly uneasy about the idea of a baby in the family but gave it little real thought. She knew she was the center of their lives; that couldn't change. And she had Scatterbrain, who was growing into an unusually affectionate cat. She was mostly white with black and tan spots on her head and tail, and she stalked after Corianne wherever she went.

Cory was almost a third-grader by then and was reading well above her grade level. Every Wednesday night the three of them walked down to the library so Cory could exchange one armload of books for another. Sometimes Daddy left them there and went farther down the street to his office to work awhile, but he always came into the library first and talked with the librarian about Cory's books, which ones she'd read over again during the week, which ones bored her.

His attention gave Cory a good, tall feeling. It proved to her that she was an important person within her world. Mom usually sat in the magazine section and contented herself with waving Cory toward the children's room, but Daddy always looked at the books she chose and commented on them. If it was a thick book with few pictures, as some of the dog stories were, he'd say, "You can handle that, Punkie, just read it slow and think about the words."

And then suddenly it all changed. Cory was wakened in the night and led away by the lady who lived next door to spend the night. Mom went to the hospital, where Cory wasn't allowed to visit, and when she came home her stomach was flat again and she was holding the new baby.

They had her hold the baby and told her she must love her new little sister, Bethy. They put on an act for her, saying they'd need her help taking care of the new baby. But they didn't even see Cory in the room; all they saw was the new baby.

Cory held the baby and sprinkled her with powder and stroked her head with her fingertip to feel the soft spot. But it was all fake. Cory knew that. They didn't need her help.

Third grade, Scatterbrain, and her library books distracted her, and Cory made the adjustment. Sometimes she even enjoyed spooning food into Bethy's mouth or wheeling her down the sidewalk in her stroller. But she longed for the old security of being the center of their family. She longed to swing again from their arms, to hug her daddy's leg and feel his hand stroking her head. But she was too big. And her parents' hands were full of strollers and diaper bags. They had no more patience for her.

After a while the baby wasn't breathing right and had to go to the doctor all the time. Allergies, they said. Scatterbrain had to go. She was taken away one day while Cory was in school, and no amount of pleading produced the truth. But Cory knew anyway. She knew about the place they called a shelter, where unwanted dogs and cats were taken and some of them killed.

She was certain then that Bethy was more loved and more important than she was.

But it wasn't cat-hair allergies after all. It was something much worse. The words for it were branded in Cory's mind. Cystic fibrosis. It meant Bethy had to stay in bed all the time and get weaker instead of bigger and stronger like normal little girls.

It meant that sympathy and compassion were demanded of Corianne. A little girl who could be jealous of a baby sister with an awful disease was a terrible person. They didn't spell it out for her in those words, but Cory understood.

And she did pity Bethy, she truly did. She made herself imagine life in a bed with no strength to move or do things for herself, and then she could pity her. But she thought, too, that Bethy was happy. Never having run or played outside, Bethy seemed absolutely content in her bed in the dining room, with toys and games and her own TV, and Mom or Daddy for company whenever she called.

It seemed to Cory that Bethy's deprivations were less than her own, but she couldn't say that to anyone, not to Daddy or Mommy or anyone. Not even to Lee.

If Bethy would die . . .

The thought drifted through her mind. Furiously she chased it away and concentrated on her own life. Fourth grade, fifth grade, skiing at Chestnut Mountain with Lee and her parents, bigger and better books to read. The Winterbottoms bought a motor home and began taking Cory with them sometimes to dog shows. It all helped.

But the hollowness, the hunger, were still there. Her parents didn't notice her; they didn't love her.

As the years passed and Bethy grew mentally but not physically, Mom became obsessed with caring for her. She'd long since given up her job at the tourism office; now she gave up her friends, her interests, and everything else. All of her attention was focused on Bethy.

Daddy started working more and more nights at Winterbottom Realty. Catching up on paperwork, he called it. Then one night he packed some clothes and drove away. He moved into a downtown apartment with one of the women from the office, and when legal things had been done, he married her.

He'd tried to explain to Cory on the first of their court-allowed weekend visits. "I'm still your daddy and I love you as much as ever," he said. Cory's mouth had twisted wryly at that. "Now I know you're too young to understand these things, Punkie, but when you get older you'll realize, well, a man has to feel needed. Your mom is a wonderful woman, but she doesn't need anything but Bethy, and I just can't take it any longer."

Cory didn't understand that part. It was Bethy who needed Mom, not the other way around.

But Cory was thirteen by then and had a hard core of self-preservation that hadn't been there when she was a little girl swinging from her parents' arms. Daddy was gone. Bethy had taken him away, just as she'd taken Scatterbrain and Mom. Cory knew by then that she hated her sister. She didn't say the words to herself, but the hate was a solid lump deep inside her. She began praying for Bethy to die. For Bethy's own good, she told God. Bethy was suffering and would be happier in heaven with him. Then Daddy would come home, and Mom would be able to focus on Cory again, hug her like she used to. They could be their old storybook family again, and go on the paddle wheeler. . . .

And then Bethy died.

And Daddy didn't come home.

And Mom didn't see Cory standing there. Mom grieved over Bethy.

And went on grieving.

Cory drew the dog tighter to her chest and rubbed her face against his.

Hour by hour Sterling's anticipation swelled. He knew where he was, where he was going. Beyond the walls of his crate were other dogs in their crates, familiar dogs. His crate vibrated to the motor noise and highway flaws. From time to time huge roars rushed past, making his crate sway lightly. When he'd had his eyes he hadn't noticed the sways from passing roars, but now he felt everything more acutely. When he couldn't touch the girl, he sometimes felt the turning of the earth, even now.

He knew where he was going, and he knew when the ride was almost over. The absence of passing roars and the smoothing of the road beneath him meant that they were coming to the final stop. There were many slowings and turnings, then a pause while the man talked to someone outside, and then the maneuvering of the motor home into its place.

Sterling stood and thrashed his tail with excitement, even though he knew it would be several minutes before he would be taken out and placed in an exercise pen. Already he could hear the distant barking of strange dogs.

At the dog shows in his memory, Sterling had felt intensely alive, staring keenly around him from his vantage point on the grooming table, seeing the exhilarating mélange of strange dogs, colorful flashing skirts, children's faces peering at him. He whined now, unable to contain his excitement. Impatiently he swiped his face against his foreleg, trying to get rid of the curtain so he could see the dogs and the swirl of show activity.

Four

The motor home was a thirty-six-foot Vista Cruiser, white with elegant narrow body stripes of blue and rose. On its roof were two air conditioners, a power-lift TV antenna, and a satellite dish. Its king-size bed, in the rear bedroom, had been replaced by built-in dog crates big enough to house the borzois. Sterling's smaller crate and the whippet's crate rode atop the borzois' huge compartments.

Usually Cory was eager to help the Winterbottoms in the setting-up process, putting up folding exercise pens with Lee, getting out food and water dishes while Todd and Trish Winterbottom rolled down the massive side awning and unreeled the electric cord.

But today, for the first time, she had her own dog. She went back to Sterling's crate and opened it while Todd was still backing the vehicle up onto its leveling blocks.

"How you doing?" she crooned. Sterling leaned against the length of her arm and laid his head on her shoulder.

"I have to go help them set up," she murmured. "I'll be right back and let you out."

He didn't whine, but he tensed and tried to hold her with his chin's pressure against her shoulder. In spite of his fear of falling he moved his body weight forward, through the crate door, and steadied himself along her arm. She wouldn't let him fall.

"Oh, okay, you can come."

She slipped his lead on and said, "Big jump." He came out joyfully, the lead supporting him and softening his landing. "Down . . . down," she said at the motor-home door, and he hopped down its two folding steps.

"Stay close," she told him and wrapped the lead swiftly around his neck to keep it from dragging and tripping him. With freed hands, Cory helped Lee drag out the exercise pens from their storage compartments under the belly of the motor home and set them up in a row, while Todd and Trish let down the side awning. Sterling moved with Cory, staying inches from her left leg.

Cory yawned as she worked. They had left Galena at three-thirty in the morning and had driven northwest for more than four hours to this south Minneapolis suburb. She had slept for an hour or so, but not enough to catch up with her need.

When the exercise pens were set up and filled with two borzois and a whippet, Cory stretched, yawned mightily, and looked around. She remembered this show building now; this was where Borowis the borzoi had won Best in Show last year. It was a sprawling high-school sports complex, low brick buildings joined by concrete walkways. Already the huge parking lot was almost filled, and cars and vans were parking along the residential streets.

"I'm going to take Sterling for a walk," Cory told Trish. The one rule on dog-show trips was to let Trish know where she and Lee were at all times. If they disappeared and Trish needed them, it made her furious.

"Get a catalog, will you?" Trish handed her a five-dollar bill. "And bring it right back. I've got to see if Natalie is here. I know she is; she wouldn't pass up a judge stack like this one . . ."

Cory escaped before Trish's mutterings became invective that demanded an audience. Lee came with her, equally anxious to escape the subject of Natalie. They walked in tandem toward the show building, Sterling trotting between them. Lee was already adept at spacing herself so that the dog fit between her leg and Cory's closely enough for body warmth and the brushing of his coat to guide him independent of the lead.

"Borowis better beat Natalie's dog for Breed this morning," Lee said, "or we're all going to have to pay. Mom'll throw our lunch plates at us." Lee chuckled.

"She'll get behind the wheel and run over Natalie with the Vista Cruiser," Cory said, "and squash her to a squish. And then the loudspeaker will say, 'Cleanup in the parking area, murder victim squashed to a squish — bring large buckets and shovels, cleanup crew.'"

They walked faster now, enjoying themselves.

Lee said, "No, no. Mom would never hit Natalie with the motor home. It cost eighty-seven thousand dollars; it might get dented. She would . . . hire some scuzzy malamute guy with a beat-up old van to do the hit-and-run for her."

Cory tightened up on Sterling's lead as they pressed through the big double doors of the building along with a flow of other exhibitors. At a table just inside the door they bought a show catalog listing the fifteen hundred entries. Lee took the catalog and change back to her mother while Cory and Sterling wandered on inside.

The huge gymnasium was filling fast with exhibitors hauling dolly-loads of crates and grooming equipment into place around the perimeter of the room. Down its center were eight rings partitioned with low white lattice fencing. In the building beyond was another gym, another clutch of rings.

Through the lead Cory could feel Sterling's tension. The dog was moving on stiffened legs, keeping himself hard against the lead and moving his head continually. She eased into a quiet space along an outside wall near the rest-room door and squatted beside him. She tried to ease him against her but the electricity in his body was almost shock level. He pulled away, whining and moving his head in scooping motions, trying to dislodge his blindness.

A young woman started past, then turned and paused before them. She was a beautifully groomed and ornamented redhead, and she led a Bedlington.

"Hi, who is this?" she said, motioning to Sterling.

"Oh, uh, he's not entered." Cory spoke softly, aware of the loosely enforced ruling against unentered dogs.

"Well, that's a relief," the woman said, grinning. "I was afraid he was going to be my competition. He's lovely. Why aren't you showing him?"

Cory felt an unexpected wash of embarrassment. She wanted Sterling to be admired, not pitied. "He's already a champion. He's from California. I just got him. He's retired from showing, he's just my pet now. I came along with my girlfriend's family; they show borzois. We're just here to watch." Too much. You're saying too much, she warned herself.

The woman knelt and ran her hand over Sterling's head. "This isn't Champion Blue Shadows Sterling, is it?"

Cory nodded. The woman stared at her.

"You're kidding. I saw him win at Beverly Hills, and at the California Specialty, and Montgomery County, and Westminster. All the biggies. And now he's just a pet? How come? This dog should be the top winner in the breed this season."

"He went blind," Cory said softly.

The woman's jaw dropped. She stared at Cory, then at Sterling's black, deep-set eyes. Tears, overflowing from the glaucoma pressure, had made brown stains under his eyes. Cory wiped his eyes continuously with cotton balls, but the chemistry of the tears caused the stains anyway.

"I'm so sorry," the woman breathed. "Was it retinal atrophy? Cataracts?"

"Glaucoma."

"What a shame. He's a lovely dog. Truly. It's too bad you can't go on showing him."

The woman left, but her words ignited Cory's imagination. Show Sterling? Why not? He would follow her around the ring. He was moving so confidently on their walks now that the judge probably wouldn't even know there was anything wrong with him.

She stood up, her mind buzzing with excitement. Not this weekend, of course. Show entries have to be gotten in weeks ahead of time, she knew. But later on? This summer? She'd be going to the shows anyway with Lee's family. It could be done.

Over the loudspeaker came the national anthem, and after that the competition began. Cory watched the Afghans in the ring before her, but she wasn't seeing Afghans, she was seeing herself and Sterling flying around that ring . . . applause . . . Sterling leaping against her in the glory of winning.

She saw herself showing his trophy to her father, to her mother. Proof. Proof that she was somebody, herself. And proof that Sterling wasn't finished.

Corianne and Sterling, together. A winning team.

All day she kept her excitement to herself. She sat in a folding chair at ringside while the Afghans finished showing and the borzois began. Windy, the Winterbottoms' bitch, was reserve winner in an entry of seven — a good placement but no points toward her championship, so Trish would count it as a bitter defeat. Then Borowis, led by Todd, sailed into the ring at the head of the line for the Best of Breed class. Behind him were two other champions, including the enemy, Natalie's dog Zhivago, and after the champions came the top-winning male and female nonchampions of the day.

Lee settled into a chair beside Cory and they leaned together tensely, silently. The tone of their weekend would be decided here; either joyful victory or miserable defeat. Borowis was the number-seven-ranked borzoi in the country this year, and if he won Best of Breed now, he stood a good chance of winning the hound group later in the day. If Borowis won the group, there was an outside chance of the biggest prize of all, Best in Show. The Best in Show judge was known to like dogs of Borowis's type.

On the other hand, Zhivago was number five in the national breed rankings and had also won under today's breed judge and group judge. There were 213 hounds at today's show. If Zhivago won the hound group it would add 212 points to his score in the national rankings and give him a dangerous lead over Borowis. If Borowis won, they'd be neck-and-neck.

Mom's over there hyperventilating," Lee murmured. "Natalie just told her Zhivago comes from this judge's breeding."

"Does he really?" Cory asked. Sterling resettled himself across her foot.

Lee shook her head. "I don't think so. Natalie was just trying to psych Mom out."

"How come your dad's handling Boro instead of her? Was she too strung out?"

"No, that's because it's a woman judge, and men handlers do slightly better under her than women handlers. Mom keeps records of stuff like that. She has a whole big fat notebook on judges. Says it gives her a competitive edge. Listen, Cor, if I ever start getting this cutthroat about any sport, dog shows or skiing or anything, would you please do me a favor and shove me off a cliff or something? I can't stand these people."

"Watch now." Cory nodded toward the ring. All the dogs had been examined and gaited. The judge, an elegantly dressed woman with a dozen gold bracelets up her arms, stood back and stared at Borowis, then Zhivago, then back to Borowis, scowling and pinching her lip.

Lee and Cory bent forward in their chairs, unable to withstand the suspense. With a motion of her hand the judge sent the dogs in one final flight around the ring, then pointed at Borowis.

The girls breathed out in unison. "Hot spit, we get steaks and champagne for supper," Lee said.

"He hasn't won the group yet," Cory reminded her. "Don't count your steaks before they hatch."

The girls stood and stretched. "Listen," Lee said, "he's already done the important thing. He beat The Enemy."

As they moved through the crowd toward the door and the motor home beyond, Corianne focused on the dog beside her.

Her own show dog.

Would she turn cutthroat herself, she wondered? If she followed Sterling into the world of competitive exhibiting, would she become like Trish and Todd?

No. She didn't need or want that. All she wanted was . . . something to show Mom. And Daddy. She wasn't Bethy, but she wasn't invisible, either. Not anymore.

Not since Sterling.

Sterling rose against the seated girl and asked admission to her lap. Settling his body against her chest, he tucked his head into the hollow of her neck. A long sigh deflated him; he lay content.

The day had been confusing for him. He was surely at a dog show, but the exciting time hadn't come. There had been no paths of fragrant rubber matting beneath him, no tension from his handler, no head-high charge around the ring with the leap of joy at the end.

There had been only the girl, leading him everywhere with her, holding him in her lap or letting him sleep across her feet. The dog shows in his memory had been all confinement in his crate except for the exciting time in the ring. Today was different, unsettling. But as long as the girl was close . . . He closed his eyes and drifted.

Five

It had been a long day for Corianne, beginning with the three A.M. wake-up, stretching through the long drive to Minnesota, the day's showing in the suburban school gym, and then the shorter drive southwest to Mankato and the setup here, for tomorrow's show.

The show building was in another sports complex, this time on a college campus. The parking lot on which they camped was surrounded by neat brick buildings, groomed lawns, and handsome landscaping. The evening was chilly, but the short-legged charcoal brazier in the center of their group gave off enough warmth for comfort, along with the fragrance of long-gone supper steaks. Beyond the brazier and lawn chairs, Borowis, Windy, and George, the whippet, lay in their exercise pens enjoying the night breeze and the stretching of legs.

As she rehearsed what she must say, Cory's heart began a thudding that disturbed Sterling's sleep. He roused and stirred against her; she stilled him with her hand.

Lee had gone inside the motor home to watch television, expecting Cory to come in with her. But Cory continued to watch Trish Winterbottom, waiting for her chance. Todd had wandered down the line to talk to someone; Trish went on with her figuring. She had been counting all of the hound entries at today's show, to compute the points Borowis had gained with his third-place win in the hound group today. She'd been figuring ever since supper and was just double-checking now.

Finally the woman said, "Yep, I was right. We got a hundred and eighty-four points today, puts Boro just thirty-one points behind that junker of Natalie's. If we can pull it off again tomorrow, hoo-boy, that bitch is going to be eating our dust."

"Um, could I ask you something?" Cory said hesitantly.

Trish looked up and focused on her, mildly surprised. "You still here? I thought you were in watching TV. Where'd Todd wander off to?"

"He's down the way there, talking to those people with the silver trailer. What I wanted to ask . . ."

She waited until Trish was focused on her again. This was too important for absentmindedness.

"What, hon?"

"Well, would you be willing to give me Sterling's registration papers?"

"Sure. Why not? What'd you want them for, though?"

Cory pulled in a nervous breath and said, "I want to show him." Her stomach knotted with anxiety. If the Winterbottoms began thinking of Sterling as having any value at all, would they want him back?

"Oh, hon, you can't show him," Trish said with the voice of authority. "He's blind."

"I know that. But he follows me just fine on the lead, and I know I could get him to show okay. . . ."

"No, Cory, I mean he's *blind*. You can't show a blind dog. It's against AKC rules. If we'd thought we could show him, we wouldn't have given him away, a dog that valuable."

"No, I guess not," Cory said faintly. "Well, guess I'll take him for a walk."

She walked Sterling on the plushy lawns of the campus, fighting disappointment as she watched him sniff and roam. She'd carried the dream for less than a day, but it had been important to her, too important to let it go easily. A victory with Sterling, a victory of some kind . . . something to show Mom that she still had a live daughter . . .

Restlessly she led Sterling back to the motor home, put him to bed in his crate, then settled beside Lee on their sofa bed to watch "The Golden Girls." Nothing of the show registered in her mind.

The television was off, the motor home silent. From the back room came soft sounds of Windy muttering in her sleep. Through the window beside her head Cory could hear voices and laughter from the next-door rig, where Trish and Todd had wandered into a spontaneous party.

Close to her ear Lee spoke. "Okay, what's up?"

"What?"

"Cory, you've been moping around here all night; you didn't even laugh at Sophia on 'Golden Girls.' You're not hearing anything I say. Do you want to tell me what's bugging you or do you want me to start guessing?"

Cory sighed. "I'll tell you, but you have to promise not to laugh at me, okay? I got this idea today, that maybe if your folks would give me Sterling's registration papers I could show him. I know, stupid idea. I asked your mom and she told me it's an AKC rule; you can't show blind dogs. Stupid rule."

"Actually it's not so stupid, when you think about it. The whole point of dog shows is to improve the quality of dogs by rewarding the best ones so people will breed from them. If a dog has something wrong with it, like blindness, he could pass it on to his offspring, so you wouldn't want dogs with unsoundnesses like that to be the big winners that everyone would be breeding to. If you follow me."

Cory thought about it. "I guess you're right. I hate it when you use logic on me, though."

Curious, Lee asked, "Why did you want to show him? What would be the point?"

Cory didn't answer.

"Cor?"

"I don't know. Stupid, I guess. I wouldn't say this to anybody but you, but, well, I've never felt like my folks loved me, you know? They were always so hung up on Bethy, and after she died I felt like it was going to be my turn. But it wasn't." Her throat swelled; her eyes dampened. She forced her voice onward. "I hate people who feel sorry for themselves," she said with low fury.

"Listen, it's okay. Personally, I think you've been getting the short end of the stick from your folks, too. Like I get with mine. That's what we have each other for, buddy."

"And Sterling." Cory's lips curved in a smile.

"And Sterling."

Cory turned her head toward Lee. "You feel like you get shafted by your folks? I never knew that. They don't seem that way to me. I mean, they do everything for you, take you everywhere with them, buy you all those gorgeous clothes that you never wear—you big jerk."

She hit Lee on the hipbone.

Lee chuckled. "They're just trying to make me pretty. It's this competitive thing they've got. You know. They have to have the biggest realty company in Galena, and sell the most expensive properties, and have the most unusual house in the home tours."

"And their dogs have to beat all their enemies' dogs," Cory said.

"Sure. That's why they go to all these dog shows in their motor home that's bigger and fancier than their enemies' rigs. They want me to be prettier than their enemies' kids, too, and I'm damned if I'm going to help them."

Cory raised onto one elbow and stared at her friend's face, outlined by the glow of the security light outside the window. "Is that why you wear your hair chopped off like it was cut with a lawn mower? And all those boring T-shirts that don't even say anything on them, when you've got such pretty stuff?"

Lee's eyes remained closed, but a wicked grin widened her cheeks. "Yeah. And besides, they think I'm going to turn out queer."

Cory's eyes widened. "You're not, are you?"

"No. Don't be a diphead. I just love that look Mom gets on her face when I do something really butch. Scares hell out of her." Lee chuckled. "So don't be surprised if they start making us sleep in separate beds on these show trips."

Cory lay back down, snorting laughter. "What separate beds? One of us would have to sleep in with them. Or on top of the kitchen counter, maybe."

"In one of the dog crates."

Their laughter died and Cory said, "You know, I hate to sound like I'm standing up for the enemy or anything, but are you sure you're being fair to them? I mean, I get a little turned off myself by all the competitive stuff they do, but I don't think that has anything to do with how much they love you. I mean, I think they really do. Love you."

"It doesn't feel like it from here." Lee's voice quavered.

The next morning Zhivago beat Borowis for Best of Breed. Zhivago was an imposing white borzoi of classic lines and undeniable showmanship, and no one seemed surprised at the win except the Winterbottoms, who stormed away from the show ring.

Cory and Lee with Sterling between them eased away from the hound ring and wandered in the other direction. In an adjoining building they found the Obedience rings and paused to watch the Utility class. A dainty sheltie was picking his way through a cluster of metal and leather articles in search of the one that held his owner's skin scent.

Suddenly Cory looked at Lee and Lee looked at Cory. "Hey," they said and looked down at Sterling.

In Cory's mind the dream mushroomed again. Sterling and her, walking victorious from an Obedience ring.

Lee said, "I bet you could show him in Obedience. They let spayed and neutered dogs compete there, so it can't be as important if the dog has things wrong with him. I'll bet you could teach him everything he'd need to know."

"Let's go watch the Novice classes," Cory said. They found chairs beside the ring in which dogs were competing in the entry-level Obedience trials. Nothing so difficult for a blind dog here, no jumping or retrieving or seeking scented articles. The dogs in this class had merely to heel, to stand without moving while the judge handled them, to come on command, and to sit and lie down in a long row of other dogs for a period of time.

"He could do all this," Cory whispered, excitement mounting. This would be even better than showing Sterling in ordinary dog-show competition, where he had already earned his championship. This would be a whole new discipline for him, much more demanding than just trotting around a show ring.

But last night's disappointment made her cautious. She turned to the man who sat on her left. He was holding two border collies, and his numbered armband marked him as an exhibitor. His expression was calm, almost bored, so he must be a seasoned Obedience exhibitor, Cory decided.

"Excuse me," she said. He turned and smiled.

"Could you tell me something?" she went on, encouraged by his smile. "I'd like to get into Obedience, but I don't know anything about it. Could you tell me if they let blind dogs compete?"

The man's smile softened to compassion. "I'm sorry, no, they don't. Blind or deaf dogs can't compete because they'd be at too much of a disadvantage. I think the rule says dogs must have useful vision and useful hearing, so if your dog is blind in both eyes, I'm afraid he would be out. Blind in one eye I'm not sure about. . . ."

"Oh. Well. Thanks. I was just wondering." Disappointment rolled over Cory, pulling her down.

Lee murmured, "Rats. Another good idea down the tubes. Listen, I'm going to go get a doughnut. You want anything?"

Cory shook her head. "No, I think I'll just wander around awhile. Whippets aren't on till eleven, right? I'll meet you at the whippet ring."

With Sterling staying as close to her leg as the best-trained Obedience dog, Corianne made her way out of the Obedience building and back into the glass-walled walkway to the main building. There was a hand-printed sign taped to the wall above the water fountain; she wouldn't have noticed it if she hadn't paused for a drink.

The sign said, Agility Demonstration, 10:00, outside main building, west lawn.

Six

Agility?

Cory stepped back for a little boy climbing the drinking fountain but went on staring at the notice. The word meant nothing to her except in the athletic sense, having a flexible body and being able to move quickly. But at a dog show?

It was a little after ten now. Curious, she went outside and found the west lawn. Sterling wanted to dawdle and sniff, but she hurried him along. They rounded the corner of the building and stopped.

An informal show ring had been set up here, with ropes looped on wooden stakes. Within the ring was what appeared to Cory to be an obstacle course, something like the horse show jumping she loved to watch on cable TV. There were jumps of various kinds, tunnels made of denim, a miniature bridge, and a structure like a steeply pitched roof, six feet tall.

A small crowd had gathered around the ring, and at the entrance a sizable group of people stood with their dogs. A man with a clipboard and stopwatch was stationed inside the ring, and a woman with a short-legged corgi stood ready at the starting line. Cory smiled to see that the starting line was marked by a pair of plastic fire hydrants.

Then she became aware of something else. Everyone around her was smiling, too, even the man with the clipboard, who appeared to be the judge. The atmosphere around this ring was different. At the rings inside the building serious wins and losses were at stake. Here, the goal seemed to be simple enjoyment.

Cory and Sterling moved closer.

"Are you ready?" the judge called, and the woman with the corgi got into a racer's semicrouch. "Yo," she boomed.

"Ready . . . set . . . GO!"

Just like kids, Cory thought.

The woman and dog spurted away from the starting line and ran straight up the middle of the ring, the dog flying over the line of jumps before him, the woman panting to keep up. At the end of the jumps they did a fast right turn and the little dog disappeared into a curved denim tunnel, reappearing almost instantly at the other end. He leaped onto the rooflike structure and scaled it, clinging and scrabbling against its cleats.

Then onto the tiny bridge, which was built to sway and dip with every step. The dog hopped off halfway across and had to go back and start over. Cory held her breath. The bridge completed, the little dog began weaving in and out through a line of ten poles. Then into another tunnel, this one open only on one end, so that he had to burrow under the fabric, a moving blue lump that emerged triumphant. At ringside, cheers.

The corgi and his handler had almost circled the ring now. Just two obstacles left, a foot-wide plank three feet off the ground and a row of hoops, like Hula Hoops, standing at angles to one another as if they were giant accordion folds. The little dog scrambled up onto the plank and trotted its length, hip-hopped through the hoops, then turned at the top of the row of center jumps and tore for home.

The crowd cheered him on with every leap; his middle-aged handler pumped her arms in a dead run to keep up with him. In a blaze of glory he shot across the finish line, barking.

Everyone laughed, Cory and the crowd and the judge. The woman opened her arms and the dog leaped into her grasp. Then attention focused on the judge, who was computing on his clipboard.

"Clear round on the obstacles," he announced. "Running time forty-nine seconds, one second over the limit, gives you a score of one-ninety-nine. Good show."

Fascinated, Cory walked around the ring to an open space and settled onto the grass to watch. Beside her Sterling strained against the lead, moving his head toward the sounds from the ring, listening and sniffing intently.

Dog after dog ran the course, shelties and Border collies and schnauzers, a tiny Yorkie, and a massive Newfoundland. Several dogs refused some obstacles; a few got excited, overshot, and had to be retrieved. But what struck Cory most forcefully was that everyone was having fun. When every dog had run and the winners were announced, no one seemed to care very much who had won or lost.

Cory wanted to go find Lee and bring her to watch, but she couldn't make herself leave, even when the demonstration was over and all that was left were a few lingering handlers, who were working their dogs over troublesome obstacles, and the judge.

Cory's thoughts raced as fast as the dogs had run around the course. With patience, Sterling could be taught to jump the jumps. And the tunnels and scaling wall and sway bridge and all the other obstacles? Could he? Could she? Would they be allowed . . . ?

She got up and made her way toward the judge, who was just finishing a conversation with the owner of a corded puli. He turned toward Cory, accustomed to waiting lines of question-askers. He was a middle-aged man, small and browned and looking more like a farmer than a dog-show exhibitor.

He looked expectantly at Cory.

"That was really fun," she said.

"Good. That's our aim. You want to get into Agility with your Bedlington, do you? Don't see many Bedlingtons, but it should be a good breed for this sport. They're fast and smart and trainable."

"He's blind," Cory said flatly.

"Oh. I'm sorry."

"Yes, but could we do it anyway? Is there a rule against blind dogs in Agility?"

"Completely blind, both eyes?"

Cory nodded, holding her breath.

"Hm. Hm, hm, hm. Don't see why not," he pronounced.

Cory's jaw dropped.

"See, Agility isn't a fully recognized AKC sport yet. It's too new, and we're still working out all the problems and setting up the rules, and of course we have to prove to AKC that there's enough interest in the sport for them to put their seal of approval on it. So at this point the rules are pretty flexible. We're just seeing what's going to work and what isn't. Now I don't know of anybody that's tried Agility with a blind dog, but I think it could be done. It would take a whole lot of time and patience on your part, and a whole lot of trust in you on your dog's part. And he probably wouldn't be able to get around the course at top speed. But I don't see why he couldn't learn to handle the obstacles. Bring him on in; let's walk him through it once. Jerry, leave it for a minute."

A blue-jeaned young man had begun picking up the obstacles and handing them to another man standing in the bed of a pickup truck backed up to the ring.

The judge put his clipboard on the grass and moved swiftly down the row of jumps, setting them all at the lowest height, a few inches above the ground. Then he came back and smiled at Cory.

"Okay, just take him over the jumps at an easy walk; let him set his own pace."

As Sterling approached the first jump, made of white plastic pipe, Cory said to him, "Okay now, up-over."

He hesitated. He knew that *up* meant a step upward, but *up-over* was a new sound. His forelegs touched the pipe. He lowered his nose and explored, then hopped easily over the low obstacle.

They walked on to the next, a fake brush jump made of green shaggy paper. "Up-over," Cory sang. Again Sterling felt the jump with his forelegs and popped over it, more quickly this time.

"Good," the judge said. "He's bright, and he trusts you."

At the next jump Sterling barely hesitated, making his jump a continuation of his walk. At the last one, Cory moved faster and gave her command a fraction sooner, and the dog made a smooth leap. He left the ground too soon but jumped so wide that he came down safely beyond the pole, then turned to jump against Cory in jubilation.

"Okay, great," the judge said, grinning in clear delight. "Let's try him on the tunnel. Hey, you guys, come watch this. This young lady is working with a blind dog here. Isn't this great?"

Cory almost laughed aloud. Among these people Sterling's blindness seemed an interesting challenge, nothing else. She felt an instant buoyancy and bent to give Sterling a quick hug. At the mouth of the tunnel she dropped his leash and said, "Come on, go through."

It was sixteen feet long, with a fairly sharp bend in the center, a denim skin stretched over metal rods to form a tunnel three feet high, a foot and a half wide.

"Go on," the judge said quickly. "You move forward so he can hear you through the tunnel. Keep talking to him."

But Sterling backed out and came to find Cory. Over and over they tried, but he wouldn't move forward without her touch on his lead. Cory's heart sank.

"Don't sweat it," someone called to her across the ring barrier. "Most of 'em balk at the tunnel, first time. You can teach him, don't worry."

The judge motioned for Cory to follow him back to his clipboard. He handed her a pamphlet and said, "Look, we've got to get our equipment out of here so they can set up for the flyball races, but here's some general information about Agility, and on the back there's the address of our Agility Association. You can send for training books, and you can call any of those phone numbers there if you need help. I'm this number right here. We'll put you on our mailing list for future demonstrations, and when your dog is ready, you can bring him. See, AKC won't let us hold Agility tests as competitions, only as demonstrations, but we treat them like competitions, with ribbons and trophies and all that. The next one that I know of will be in Saint Paul in June, and then there's one at Rochester in September."

"Thanks," Cory said. The word was inadequate, but she knew no way to tell him what he'd given her.

"Where were you?" Trish demanded with ill-concealed anger. "You were supposed to meet us at the whippet ring at eleven, and it's almost noon. We're all loaded and ready to go; we were just waiting for you."

"I'm sorry," Cory said. "I went over and watched the Agility demonstration, and . . ."

"Never mind, just get in. We've got to get on the road. Wasted enough time in this damned place."

Cory climbed into the motor home and slammed the door as Todd started the engine. She glanced at Lee, who winked. Balancing against the sway of the floor, she took Sterling back to his crate and lifted him in, then plopped onto the sofa beside Lee. They each sat at an end, facing each other, arms along the sofa back, window beside them. Their feet nestled together from old habit.

Todd and Trish were a safe distance away beyond the kitchen, and the roar of the diesel engine gave the girls privacy to talk.

Cory grimaced in the direction of Lee's parents. "I take it George didn't cover himself with glory, judging from the mood up there."

"George got dumped. Fifth out of five, so Mom was the only one in the class who had to walk out without a ribbon, and you know what that does to her sunny disposition. God, she hates fifth out of five. She wasn't really mad at you. Heck, we just finished loading when you got here, so you weren't holding us up. She's just got to yell at somebody. Hey, shall we make peanie-butter sandwiches? I'm starved."

Cory was, too, suddenly. With their sandwiches on paper towels, and cans of cold pop from the refrigerator and a nearly full bag of chocolate-chip cookies between them, they settled onto the sofa again.

"I was watching the Agility demonstration," Cory said. "Did you ever see it?"

"Never heard of it." Lee's words were blurred with peanut butter.

Cory's eyes shone. "It's what Sterling and I are going to do," she announced.

Sterling woke and lifted his head to listen. There were no sounds yet of the girl's coming, but it was time.

He lay on her bed in the luxury of her scent. Until today he had spent the daytime hours in his crate for its security, waiting for the girl to come. Today, for the first time, he'd crept out and jumped up onto the bed where he slept at night.

Downstairs the front door opened, stayed open a moment, then closed. Sterling sat up, head cocked. Whining softly, he found the edge of the bed and eased off it, then put his nose to the floor. The path of densest scents lay to the right and led through the door, along the hallway, then down the stairs. Like a train following its track, Sterling negotiated the stairs by keeping to the center of the dense scent trail and stepping down at each point where the scent grew abruptly distant by several inches.

The living room held a wafting of her scent. His mind carried a map of the room and its obstacles, so he moved across the open space before him, toward the television set, on which the girl's schoolbooks had just been piled. Gracefully he rose on his hind legs and sniffed the books, then sat before the television to wait for her.

Seven

Cory looked around the yard and smiled. Her mood was a blend of satisfaction, excitement, and anticipation. Last night after the show trip she'd lain awake in bed, planning everything, and now it was beginning to take shape.

Her mother had been watching television when Cory had come home from the Winterbottoms'. It was nearly dark then, too dark to explore the contents of the tiny detached garage behind the house.

Taking courage in hand, Cory had turned off the television and sat on the footstool in her mother's line of vision.

"Hey, I was watching that," Nan Wendel said. She was in her powder-puff bathrobe and bunny slippers again, almost ready to go upstairs to bed.

"I've got something important to tell you, Mom. Can you listen a minute? I'll turn it back on then."

Nan moved forward slightly. It was so seldom that her silent daughter asked for attention. "Is something wrong? Did something happen?"

"No, yes. Nothing wrong, something happened. Mom, at this show today they had a new sport that I'd never heard of, called Agility, where the dogs have to run around a course and go over jumps and through tunnels and stuff like that, and they time them and the fastest clean round wins. It was so exciting, I just loved it. And I talked to the judge afterwards; he was really nice, and he said a blind dog could do it! He said there wasn't any rule against blind dogs, and if I had the patience and took the time to teach Sterling, he could probably do it. So I want to, okay?"

"But why?" Nan said, puzzled. Part of her mind was still following the movie she'd been watching.

"Because there's rules against blind dogs in regular dog-show classes and Obedience. I checked. And I want to do something with Sterling, Mom."

"But why? Isn't it enough just to have him for a pet and love him? Isn't that why you got him?"

Cory choked on the pressure of words she couldn't say.

"Honey," Nan went on, "I don't care. If it's something you really want to try, I don't see any harm in it, but I just hope you're not catching all that competitive zeal from the Winterbottoms. Like your dad has, with the real estate. I know Lee isn't like that, and I don't think you are, but you and I both know Todd and Trish can get pretty cutthroat. Their business . . ."

Cory's father seemed suddenly to be present in the room with them. Working for the Winterbottoms had changed him; Nan knew it and Cory sensed it. His integrity had begun crumbling around the edges under pressure to make a sale, bring in the commissions, edge out the competitors.

"No, it's not that," Cory said. "That's one good thing about Agility, Mom. Those people were having fun with their dogs, and they cheered each other on. Really cheered. It wasn't like the Winterbottoms at all. Can I do it?"

Nan looked fondly at her daughter, and Cory warmed in her mother's gaze.

"I don't care. Give it a try if you want. He's your dog."

"Will you help? I need to build a training course just like they had at the show. I've got the address to send to for building instructions. Some of it's going to cost some money, but I was thinking I might be able to work Saturdays at the dog-grooming place and make enough to pay for what I need to buy."

Nan said, "You're already working Saturdays at the grooming place for nothing. You think your boss is going to be willing to start paying you for what you're already doing free?"

Cory shook her head, frustrated by the difficulty of explaining important things to her mother. "I'm trading off. Two dog baths for an hour's use of her clippers and combs and scissors and stuff. We have it all figured out. But Iva told me she gets a lot busier in the summer, with summer people's dogs, and I kind of had the feeling she might take me on part-time after school gets out. She likes me."

"So what's the problem?"

"It's not a problem," Cory explained, "it's just that I don't want to have to wait till school gets out to start building my training course. I want to get started right away, tomorrow, and I was thinking maybe there was some junk in the garage that I could make a few jumps with if you don't care."

"Use anything you want. I don't care. Now can we please have the movie back on?"

Cory rose, hesitated, then bent to touch her mother's cheek with a swift kiss. It startled both of them.

Now Cory stood on the front lawn, smiling in satisfaction at the pile on the grass before her: a rake, a broken hoe handle, chunks of two-by-four lumber, a clutch of empty oil cans. Perfect.

She spun and ran up the steps and pulled open the front door. Sterling was sitting like a statue in the living room, near where she'd deposited her schoolbooks on the television. He rose and came to her, wriggling with joy. When he knew her distance he leaped at her chest.

"Sterling! You got out of your crate! You came downstairs all by yourself. Fantastic. You're wonderful—I love you. Come on, we'll go OUT now."

She snagged his lead from the coat hook by the door and led him "down . . . down . . . down" into the front yard. When he'd relieved himself Cory slipped the lead off.

"Now I've got work to do. Can you stay with me, without your lead?" She moved toward the pile on the grass; Sterling walked beside her, somewhat stiff-legged but following her scent and the sound of her shoes in the grass.

On the part of the lawn that was the most level, Cory set up a circle of miniature jumps: the rake, which rose only a few inches above the ground; the hoe handle, set across a pair of oil cans; and a two-by-four a few feet long, also propped up on oil cans. Looking at the jumps, Cory thought, More would be better. And I'll have to get higher ones. But this will do to get him started, find out if he really can do it.

"Okay, pupper, we're going to try this now. Here, we'll put your lead back on so I can help you, and then pretty soon you'll be doing it on your own. Okay. Here we go. Sterling, GO."

She moved him forward in a trot, into the ring of jumps and straight at the rake handle. One step away from it she said, "Ster, OVER."

He hesitated, knocked against the rake handle with his forefoot, and hopped across it.

The hoe-handle jump was about eight inches high. Again she said "Over" just as the dog approached it. This time he lowered his head to locate the object with his nose, then hopped across it. He did the same at the third jump, which was slightly higher.

Around the circle they went again, Cory concentrating on her timing. It was crucial, she knew, to give him the *over* command at just the right instant, leaving time for it to be processed through his mind and into his legs.

At first Sterling hesitated and dropped his nose at each jump, but after several rounds he began to rely on Cory's voice rather than on his own senses. He learned the pattern of the circle, knew when a jump was coming up, listened for her command, and took off on that instant.

"Yes!" Cory whooped finally, and rolled on the ground with him in a wrestling hug. "You can do it. We're going to do it, old buddy. You and me, we're going to show them."

When Nan came home from work Cory made her watch from the front steps while she took Sterling over the course three times. He leaped perfectly at every jump, sailing far higher than the tiny jumps required.

"That's good, honey. You can see Sterling really trusts you. What do you want for supper? Chili sound okay to you?"

Her mother's praise was miniature compared to Cory's own excitement, but it was something.

The next afternoon Cory gave up precious training time to walk Sterling down the brick sidewalks to Iva's shop.

On the grooming table in the back room was a mammoth Old English sheepdog lying on his side, sound asleep. The front half of his right side was peeled down to an inch of bright white and blue-gray wool; the rest of him was solid mats six inches thick. They rolled slowly away before Iva's clippers and dropped with muffled thuds to the floor.

"Wow," Cory breathed.

Moving her lips in an odd rippling motion, Iva maneuvered her cigarette from the center to the corner of her mouth and said, "This is Hairy. Hairy comes in once a year for a shave-down, whether he needs it or not. Takes a good six hours, and I charge 'em seventy-five bucks, and they keep bringing him back. Year after year. Forever. Always ruin at least two blades on old Hairy, don't I, boy?"

She lifted a mat to peer at Hairy's eye, but it was closed. He snored lightly.

"I was wondering . . . ," Cory said.

With a curse at her overheating clippers, Iva laid them aside and went at Hairy's foreleg with her shears. "What."

"I need some money and I was wondering if I could work here maybe part-time? Maybe this summer? I mean, like, for money?"

An oath escaped Iva's lips, as her shears nipped a tiny bloody V in Hairy's shoulder. He slept on. "Yeah, okay," she said. "You're not as rotten as most kids. I can stand to have you around."

Cory grinned.

"You can start working Saturdays if you want, eight till four, doing baths and comb-outs and whatever else I tell you to, okay? Three dollars an hour, cash, no withholding tax nor nothing. I ain't going to waste my time on all that federal tax-form stuff."

Elation welled in Cory. "Can I still groom Sterling here?"

Iva squinted over Hairy's body and ground out her cigarette in an overflowing saucer. "Kid drives a hard bargain. Yeah, but not on my time. Come early or stay late if you want to work on your own dog. Fair?"

"Fair. Now ask me what I need the money for." Cory was bursting to tell her.

"You're gonna run away from home. You're pregnant. You need money for your drug habit."

"Get serious. I'm going to build a training course and teach Sterling to do Agility, and then I'm going to compete in an Agility trial with him."

Iva stopped snipping and stood up. The silence roused Hairy, who lifted his massive, matted head and stared at Cory as though accusing her of interrupting his beauty treatment. Then he sighed, shifted to a more comfortable position on the table, and went back to sleep.

"What the heck is Agility, and how can you do it with a blind dog?"

Cory explained.

When she finally ran down, Iva shrugged and said, "I think you're crazier than a hoot owl, girl. But I like your guts. You get him trained to do all that stuff and I'll come and dance at your dog show."

The first Saturday at the shop seemed endless to Cory. She started work at eight and spent four solid hours standing beside a raised bathtub, shampooing and rinsing dog after dog. Augie, the Cocker from Hell, was one of her first bathees and he bit her twice on the hand before she managed to get him muzzled. After that he submitted almost cheerfully to the sudsing and spray-rinsing.

Most of the dogs were well behaved. There were two schnauzers, a poodle, three Lhasas, and a bearded collie, all before lunch. Cory was not at all sure she'd make it through the afternoon. She sat on a stool in a corner of the grooming room to eat her sandwiches at the noon break, while Iva went upstairs to her apartment for a hot lunch and a quick nap.

In the afternoon Cory bathed four more dogs, then worked on comb-outs. Iva even let her run the clippers over the back and sides of one of the schnauzers. By the end of the day Cory had a backache, two dog bites, itchy skin from clippered dog hair that had worked through her clothing, and almost twenty-five dollars.

Cory ordered an Agility book from the address the judge had given her at Mankato. He had told her the book included instructions for building the obstacles, as well as training tips and rules for competition.

The Winterbottoms were gone almost every weekend now on dog-show trips, but Cory stayed at home, spending Saturdays at Iva's shop and Sundays training Sterling over the rake jump, the hoe handle, and anything else she could find to serve as jumps.

Sterling seemed to enjoy the training sessions. He grew tense with concentration when she led him to the front lawn, and he leaped with joy when the lesson was successfully completed. To Cory, he appeared hungry for her praise and happy to learn her lessons in order to earn it. And she knew he loved the jumping. As his confidence in her voice commands grew, so did the height of his leaps.

In early May the Agility book finally arrived and Cory was able to begin buying the materials and constructing the first of the obstacles. Time was tight now. She dared not neglect her homework and she would not neglect Sterling. Saturdays were eaten up by the grooming shop; after-school daylight hours were spent with Sterling, walking him, romping with him, working him over the jump course. Evenings were for homework. That left only Sundays for construction.

Sundays were supposed to be her days with her father and Diana, his new wife, in his home in one of the old downtown hotels that had been renovated into charming apartments. But neither Cory nor Ron Wendel had remained true to the court order. Sundays were busy working days for Ron, showing quaint old brick cottages to wealthy Chicagoans in search of weekend homes. And often Cory had gone on show trips with the Winterbottoms.

On the first Sunday after the arrival of the Agility book Cory met her father on the front steps when he came to pick her up. "Daddy, would you care if I didn't come to the apartment today? I got my instruction book this week for the Agility course I was telling you about. Mom took me to the lumberyard Friday night and we got this PVC pipe, and I really want to get started on building this stuff. Okay?"

He tried not to look relieved. "Well if that's what you want to do today, sure, go ahead. PVC pipe, huh? What are you going to do with that?" He wandered toward the pile of white plastic pipe near the sidwalk and nudged it with his toe.

Cory pulled in a big breath. "I'll make jumps out of this two-inch pipe here. I can cut it with a hand saw, but can I borrow your electric drill to drill holes in it? See, I've got these corner fittings in this box here, and I'll glue it together, bases and uprights, and I'll drill holes in the uprights and put these pegboard hooks in the holes. And then I'll cut this one-inch-wide pipe into three-foot lengths and use those for the crossbars, lay them on the hooks in the uprights — and I can raise and lower the height of the jump just by putting the crossbars on higher hooks, see?

"And then this four-inch-wide pipe, I'll cut that into four pieces four feet long to make the pause box that Sterling has to jump into and sit in for five seconds. This other one-inch pipe I'll cut into ten three-foot lengths, and I'll stick them in cans of wet cement, and those will be the weave poles. We got a bag of ready-mix cement, see. And that one-by-twelve board, that's for the teeter-totter. Those two doors over there, those will be the scaling wall. Then I have to get stuff to make the tunnels with, and more lumber for the sway bridge, but I ran out of money. A couple more Saturdays at the shop and I can get everything I'll need."

Ron looked at his daughter quizzically. "You really think you can do all that?"

"Yes," she said clearly, meeting his eye.

He grinned. "Good for you. Listen, we can just let the Sunday visits go for now. I can see you've got your hands full with this project. Tell you what, I've got to meet some people at a listing at ten this morning, but I should have some free time after lunch. I'll bring over the drill."

Cory grinned back.

"Go . . . over . . . over . . . yay!"

Sterling's joy mounted with each leap. When he ran in this circle, led by the girl's voice, he felt freed from the curtains in his eyes. The girl's voice told him he could run safely, told him when to leap. As long as she was there, just beyond the right side of his head, he could move almost without caution.

She was the part of him that replaced his eyes.

Her joy in this new game stirred the instinct at the bottom of his brain, that same instinct that guides sled dogs and stock dogs and guard dogs. This was it. This was what he was here for, to do this job. The girl's laughing voice was at the center of his soul.

Eight

That afternoon Ron brought back with him not only his electric drill but also his power saw and Diana. She and Nan had reached a point of reasonable comfort in each other's presence, although they avoided unnecessary closeness.

Diana was strikingly pretty, with long caramel-colored hair in windblown waves and a tanning-parlor tan, but today the expensive boutique casual clothes were replaced by denim shorts and a tank top. She emerged from the station wagon with a carton in her arms.

"Can you use these for your pole bases?" she asked, sending an uneasy smile toward Nan as she lowered the carton for Cory's inspection. Inside it were a dozen black plastic plant pots a foot high, the kind shrubbery from the nursery comes in.

Cory had been working all morning on the base for the teeter-totter. Hand-sawing the plastic pipe and glueing the curved fittings had gone more slowly than she'd expected. Although her vision had been to build the equipment all by herself, she quickly realized the advantages of extra hands and power tools. In less time than it had taken her to saw through one piece of pipe her father had zipped off all ten of the thirty-inch lengths for the weave poles, and six crosspieces for the jumps.

Diana and a somewhat reluctant Nan went to work on solving the problem of how to hold ten pieces of plastic pipe upright in pots of wet cement until the cement dried enough to support them. Finally Nan produced a length of old clothesline rope, which the women looped from the porch rail to the Russian olive tree and twisted together. Then, laughing more freely, they mixed the cement and poured it into the ten pots, stuck the pipes in, and arranged them in a row beneath the ropes, working the tops of the pipes into the twisted ropes for support.

While they worked on the weave poles, Sterling lay on the warm bricks of the steps and enjoyed the sounds and scents of the activities around him. Cory and Ron cut and drilled and measured and glued until they had bases and uprights for six jumps assembled and drying.

"Now," Ron said as they settled in lawn chairs for beer and pop, "where do you think you're going to set up all this stuff?"

Cory waved toward the front yard, where the makeshift jumps stood. "Out there, I guess. I'll have to work around the trees, and the ground isn't very level, but . . ."

"I don't think that's going to work." Ron shook his head. He'd been studying the course layouts in the Agility book. "You're going to need more space than that, someplace without all those big trees in the way. And without that slope. You set a course sixty feet long in this yard, and you're going to be getting off into that downhill corner over there."

"I know it, but . . ." Cory tried not to whine. She was grateful for his and Diana's help with the building jobs, but she didn't want them taking over any more of the project than that. And she had already realized that the yard wasn't going to work, not for a full-sized training course.

"I know," Diana said suddenly. "How about Holyrood House? That back garden? Maybe Cory could take over the mowing for the summer in exchange for the use of that lower part of the garden. Workable?"

Cory stared at her father. Holyrood House would be incredibly, fantastically perfect.

It was her father's most valuable and most unsalable listing. He'd been trying for three years now to sell it, but its owner, a Milwaukee dowager, wouldn't lower the price to a reasonable level. It stood empty and unused year after year, except for the Galena tours of historic homes each spring and fall, when it was cleaned and opened to the public.

Her father squinted at her, fingering his gold neck chain thoughtfully. "I don't know. Could you handle the mowing job, do you think? The estate isn't going to try to keep up the gardens this year; they'll just have the landscaper clear out the beds once a month and trim things back. If they didn't have to mow the grass it'd save the estate some money there. I don't think the owner would object to your using that lower garden. No one will go there now till the fall home tour unless we get a prospective buyer."

"Fat chance," Diana muttered.

"I can do the mowing," Cory said breathlessly. "Let's go over and look at it now, can we?"

"No, we can't," Diana said to Ron in a warning voice. "We're supposed to be at the country club in fifteen minutes, in case you forgot, and I've got to get cleaned up and changed, and so do you."

"Oh. Right. I did forget. Here, Cor." He fished a mammoth ring of keys from his pocket and located a small brass key. "This is to the back gate, the one off the footpath. That'll be closest for you. You can check it out and let me know if you want to use it, okay? If you do, call me tonight so I can get the lawn service canceled."

The footpath began near the sidewalk just three houses down from Cory's and tunneled through dense greenery for fifty yards, ending at an ornate wrought-iron gate. With Sterling sniffing beside her Cory opened the gate and stopped at the edge of the clearing beyond it.

Just before her lay an oval of level green lawn framed by trees and brush. Along the far edge was a stone retaining wall that rose to the level of the next garden, formally laid out in flower beds and graveled paths. Beyond that stood the mass of rosy bricks and dark timbers and slate roofs that was Holyrood House. It belonged in seventeenth-century England, or at least on the cover of a romance novel.

Cory knew from the years when her mother had been a gowned hostess on home tour weekends that the house had been built by a French fur trader who had made millions in the beaver trade, buying pelts from the Indians and selling them to the Europeans for beaver hats. He'd been murdered by a rival, an Englishman, who took over not only the beaver trade but the Frenchman's mansion, his wife, and at least two of his mistresses. He'd renamed the mansion Holyrood House and settled in to eventual respectability. The Milwaukee dowager who was the mansion's present owner was a descendent of a legitimized son of one of the murderer's mistresses.

None of that was important to the girl who stood at the edge of the clearing, a silver dog at her side. She saw the green oval of the lower garden as her proving ground, hers and Sterling's. Here they would master the obstacle course or give up on it. One or the other.

Two weeks later Cory and Sterling stood again at the garden entrance. But now the garden had been transformed. Curious structures ringed the grassy floor; a row of white plastic-pipe hurdles ran lengthwise up the center of the oval. Around the edge was a four-foot square outlined in fat white pipe, a roof-shaped scaling wall made of two doors hinged together at the top, a low bridge that swayed in the middle, a line of ten poles in cemented plant pots, set at two-foot intervals, a long cloth tunnel with a bend in its middle, a yard-high "dog walk" made of a board just ten inches wide, with ramps leading on and off, a short tunnel whose fabric fell to the ground at one end, a low teeter-totter, and seven Hula Hoops standing upright fastened together in a long zigzag.

Cory looked at it all and sighed with satisfaction. It had taken every bit of her dog-bathing income and all of her spare time for the past two weeks. It had taken all her energy this morning to haul it all from home in the neighbor's wheelbarrow down the sidewalk, along the footpath, and through the iron gate. But there it was.

There it was, and it was good. The jumps were solid. The bridge and scaling wall and teeter-totter were painted dark green for beauty and weather protection.

Now the real work would begin, the exciting work.

It was a warm, muggy afternoon, but neither girl nor dog was aware of discomfort as they approached the starting mark, a pair of rocks Cory had set in the grass. This first part would be easy, she thought. Sterling already jumped on command.

First she walked him over the length of the oval, letting him step over the strange jumps. Then they went back to the starting rocks and turned to face the course.

"Sterling, ready, set, GO." They trotted forward, the dog's head erect with attention. "Ready, over . . . over . . . over . . . over." He negotiated the jumps stiffly, unsure of himself in this strange setting.

With her hand on his collar Cory led him to the end of the teeter-totter plank. She patted the wood and coaxed him to step up onto it. Reluctantly he edged forward, up the slope, leaning harder and harder against her hand. Suddenly the board beneath his feet sank away. Panic gripped him, and dizziness. He leaped sideways, landed in a scramble, ran a few yards away from the thing and crashed into the edge of the scaling wall.

"Oh, Sterling, come here, it's okay. It's all right, pupper. I'm sorry; that was my fault. I should have steadied it for you till you got used to it. You're okay now, quit shaking. Here, come here."

She tried to cradle him against her, but he was stiff with fear. She slipped his lead back on and gradually coaxed him into a walk. Around and around the outside of the course they walked, slowly, while the stiffness left his legs and neck. When at last he was walking normally and wagging his tail, she led him over the flight of jumps again, slowly.

"We'll leave the climbing stuff for later," she said. "You can do the pause box, though, I bet."

At the four-foot square of fat pipe she gave him the *over* command, then immediately said, "Sit." He didn't know the word, so Cory eased him down into a sitting position and steadied him there for a count of five. Again and again they practiced, and soon his rump began descending on the word *sit*.

Once more down the line of jumps they went, a little faster this time, then through the gate and home.

Lee was waiting for her when she got there. Lately they hadn't seen much of each other outside of school. Lee's weekends had been taken up by dog show trips and Cory's by the grooming-shop job and obstacle building. Cory had kept Lee up to date on the Agility project over school lunches and in evening phone calls, but they'd had little time together.

Now, this first day of summer vacation, they smiled at each other like long-separated family.

"Come on down and see it," Cory said, and they went back down the block, through the woods, and into the mansion's back garden. They walked the course, Cory explaining and Lee admiring.

"Boy, I wish I had a dog I could do this stuff with," Lee said. "This really looks like fun."

"Maybe George or Windy?"

Lee shook her head. "Mom would never let me mess around with their valuable show dogs. You were so lucky Sterling went blind."

Startled, Cory looked at her. "I guess, if you think of it that way. Lucky for me but not for him."

"Oh, I don't know. He's got a better life now than he would have had at our place, living in a crate all the time, even if he could see. What's to see inside a dog crate? He's better off with you than with vision."

Cory cocked her head and said thoughtfully, "Yeah. Maybe so."

She ran Sterling over the jumps and into the pause box. "That's all he can do so far. I tried him on the teeter-totter and he about freaked out. Jumped off and scared himself silly. It's going to take a long time to get him used to that, I guess."

Lee studied the teeter-totter. "What if we got him between us and kind of steadied him from both sides?"

"That might work better, but I don't want to try it today, while he's still remembering his fear. I thought I'd start on the less scary stuff till he gets his confidence back. You could come over and help if you want. Oh, I forgot to tell you. Iva said I could work at the shop on weekday mornings now that school's out. I guess she's a lot busier with all the summer people's dogs to do, and the kid she had working for her last summer is working at Hardees this year. So that'll give me some money for Sterling's eye medicine and for show entries later on when he gets trained, and I'll still have afternoons for training him."

Lee hung her head and said in a deep voice, "Does this mean no swimming all summer? No loafing? No reading books all afternoon? No hanging out downtown?"

"You got it."

Lee considered. "I'll help when you need help, okay? And the rest of the time I'll be swimming, loafing, reading, and hanging out."

They laughed and headed home.

"Ready . . . set . . . GO!" Sterling moved forward at the girl's voice. It held him on course and pulled him along like a leash against his neck. "Over," and "Over," again and again down the length of the course. After the fourth jump he veered to the right and slowed, dreading what came next.

Her fingers tapped on wood; he gathered his courage and stepped gingerly, his feet touching the narrow board that sloped upward toward the falling place.

Her voice urged him on. He had to do it. He made himself lean forward against the dark and begin the climb. Cautiously he crept up, fighting the dizziness.

"Slow," she cautioned.

He balanced back on his legs and stiffened as the board sank beneath him. It took all his courage not to jump, not to let the dizziness knock him sideways to the ground.

The board bumped to a stop. With a rush he skittered down the slope to the unmoving ground. Ecstatic, he ignored the next obstacle and ran toward the girl's cheering voice. He needed a hug, and he got it.

Nine

The summer rolled past, days and weeks disappearing from the wealth of time June had promised. In July a record-breaking heat wave moved in and stayed. Temperatures of a hundred degrees slowed everyone—tourists, children, joggers—to a walk.

The grooming shop wasn't air-conditioned, but giant fans kept the back room bearable, and Cory's bathing job kept her pleasantly damp most of the time. But that was only mornings. The afternoons were supposed to be training time, but the heat was so oppressive that Cory didn't have the heart to force herself or Sterling out into it. They stayed in the house, Cory reading, Sterling napping with his paw or his head across her leg.

So evenings became training time, although two evenings a week were lost to lawn mowing. The home lawn was Cory's responsibility, and now there was the huge

Holyrood House lawn to do. The lawn grass itself was dormant in the heat, but the weeds and rough grasses grew on. Mowing the training course meant moving aside all of the obstacles, uprooting the metal rods that supported the tunnels, and pounding them back in again afterward.

But the rest of the long summer evenings, after early suppers, gave Cory and Sterling a comfortable two hours' worth of training time. At first their progress was fast and exciting. Almost every night there was visible improvement in Sterling's confidence. He learned to jump high and wide and exactly on cue, and Cory learned the precise instant to give the command, watching both the jump and Sterling's stride. She called "Over" just as his forelegs were coming down at the end of the gallop stride, so that he could gather himself for takeoff instantly.

The open tunnel proved to be no real problem. Once Sterling became familiar with the scent of the tunnel fabric he trotted right through. It was the voice he followed; he didn't know Cory was hidden behind the tunnel wall.

The closed tunnel bothered Sterling at first. When his face hit the fabric barrier he stopped dead, afraid he would walk into pain. But Cory's hand reached through, touched him, and showed him how to lower his head and follow her fingers under the loosely closed end of the tunnel. After several attempts he no longer hesitated.

The smell of cement and plastic pots told him he was approaching the line of weave poles. Here Cory slipped on his lead and guided him, chanting, "Out, in. Out, in. Out, in," as she steered him left and right. After a few weeks Cory knew that Sterling was following her words, not the lead, and tried taking him through the poles off lead. "Out, in. Out, in," she chanted, and Sterling made his cautious way around the poles.

The scaling wall presented its own difficulty. It was made of two wooden doors hinged together at the tops and covered with rubber matting and narrow wood strips. Cory had spread its base wide apart so that the climb was a gentle one, and Sterling mastered it in just a few lessons. But as she steepened the angle of the climb, Sterling was unable to claw his way up. He needed run-on speed, she knew. The slow walk at which he approached the obstacle simply didn't give him the necessary impetus to propel his body up the wall.

Reluctantly Cory lowered the obstacle to a gentler slant and concentrated on building speed on the approach. "Fast UP," she called as soon as he came off the teeter-totter, and she ran ahead of him to urge him forward. He gained speed as his confidence built.

The hardest obstacles for Sterling were the raised balancing obstacles: the teeter-totter, the swaying bridge, and the dog walk with its narrow high plank. Cory left those for last, building Sterling's confidence on the jumps, the pause box, the tunnels, the weave poles, and the hoops.

Cory and Sterling were both frustrated by Sterling's lack of vision, especially with the problem of getting around the course. He could follow the sound of Cory's voice and the swish of her feet in the grass, but he was imprecise. Sometimes he angled away from the line of travel and knocked against a jump's uprights or the edge of the tunnel's mouth. In the early stages of the training Cory had led him to each obstacle, but to run the course for competition she knew she couldn't use the lead. The dogs they'd be competing against would be able to see the obstacles and would be able to negotiate them with speed and precision. Sterling would have only her voice for guidance.

After the dog had learned the *out-in* commands for the weave poles Cory began to experiment with voice commands. She called "Out" to guide Sterling away from her and "In" to steer him toward her. At first the words confused him; he stopped and sniffed the cement in the plastic pots. But after many lessons and much gentle pushing or pulling on his collar, the connection was firm in his mind.

After that they worked on simple navigation for at least half of every training period. Going at an easy jog-trot away from the obstacle course with Sterling close beside her, Cory would call "Out," sending the dog at a tangent away from her. "In" would angle him back in her direction. His line of travel was often wavering, especially when he worked at a distance from her, but with endless patience and practice Cory was able to send him, seemingly by remote control, around and across every gravel path in the upper garden, up and down the timbered steps between the upper and lower levels, and around the Agility course.

The training sessions weren't all solitary. Early in the summer Lee came often, to help. At first her presence was welcome and natural, but in late June she began arriving on the back of Nathan Crouse's Honda, and that changed everything. Nathan was a stranger in their tight circle, an intrusion. His voice was too loud. He spooked Sterling. He made jokes about things that were dead serious to Cory and took a condescending attitude toward the whole business. To him, a dog on a teeter-totter was hilarious.

After a few evenings with Nathan in the clearing, Lee understood. She came alone, on her bike, and didn't bring up the subject of Nathan unless Cory asked.

But she was still hanging out with him. Cory knew that. It was the situation both of them had foreseen, and talked about over the last couple of years: the first boyfriend. It was bound to happen to one of them before it happened to the other, and privately Cory had been braced for the worst, for being the left-behind, the left-out.

It was happening now, and yet she was detached, unhurt after all. Sterling was the center of her world, for now. Sterling and the Agility course. It was enough.

There were other visitors too, on those hazy blue summer evenings. Dad and Diana came by on Wednesday nights after their golf afternoons at the club. Dad's interest centered on the course obstacles, how the bracing was holding up under the dog walk, and whether there should be rain-drain holes in the denim tunnel tops.

Diana at first stood, almost shyly, on the sidelines, watching. One night Cory asked her to steady Sterling on the other side of the dog-walk ramp, and after that Diana was quick to step in. When Cory thanked her she looked warmly pleased.

Sometimes Nan wandered down the street to watch. She was less help than Dad and Diana, but her presence gave Cory a buzz of excitement. Nan was the important audience, to be played to and impressed.

On the nights when Dad, Diana, and Nan all showed up, Cory sensed a subtle competitive spirit in her mother. Nan jumped to help Cory a split second before Diana could get to the dog walk or the teeter-totter, to steady Sterling's off-side. Secretly Cory grinned and enjoyed it.

One night in early August the audience grew by one. Cory glanced away from her "remote control" practice to see someone new on the grassy bank between Nan and Diana. It was Iva, cigarette bouncing at the corner of her mouth. Cory maneuvered Sterling along a garden path, around a rose tree, and back toward her, using varying pitches of the voice commands *in, out*, and *down* to bring him down the timbered steps from the upper garden.

"Good night, nurse!" Iva exclaimed.

"So what do you think? Cory asked. She assumed they'd all introduced themselves to each other.

"Never seen anything like that in my life," Iva said.

Cory glowed.

Iva turned to Nan and elbowed her. "You ever seen anything like that in your life?" Nan shook her head, smiling.

"Listen," Iva said loudly, "I used to do a good bit of Obedience training in my day, before my lungs went bad. Dog hair. I got big wads of dog hair in my lungs, did you know that?"

Nan and Diana shook their heads, fighting grins, while Ron gazed away at the trees, his face carefully controlled.

"It's the God's truth," Iva swore. "You groom dogs forty some-odd years like I been doing, you breathe in a lot of teeny little bits of dog hairs, not to mention all that spray and gunk. Doc says I got dog-groomer's lungs. Told me twenty years ago to get out of the business or I'd be dead in another ten, but hell, I love doing it and I already outlived two doctors. I'm too ornery to die."

"Wads of dog hair, huh?" Nan said faintly.

"Yeah, so I quit all that dog-training stuff. That's hard work. Hell, I used to work tracking dogs, field trial dogs, utility obedience, everything. Even did terrier trials with this cairn I had. So I know what I'm talking about here. This kid has worked a miracle with that little old blind Bedlington and you folks don't even know it. Hell, she probably don't even know it herself."

Cory grinned till her cheeks ached.

Taking out her cigarette to wave it for emphasis, and nearly setting Nan's hair on fire, Iva commanded, "Let's see him go over them jumps there, kid."

And when Sterling had completed his run, Iva jammed her cigarette back into her mouth for a solid round of applause, cupping her palms for louder noise.

Although Cory enjoyed her audiences, it was the nights when she and Sterling worked alone, or with Lee, that they made the most progress. Gradually Sterling mastered each of the obstacles, even the climbing ones, except for the sway bridge and the teeter-totter, which continued to frighten him. Reluctantly he would step onto the board, and more reluctantly climb it, until it began to sink beneath his feet. Then he panicked and leaped off, unless hands and bodies steadied him from both sides.

It wasn't until a night in late August, when the evening-blue air was alive with lightning bugs, that Sterling finally climbed the board to its fulcrum, rode it down to its jarring stop, and trotted off unaided.

Ignoring Cory's jubilant command, "Fast-UP," for the scaling wall, he ran to her and leaped into her arms for a hug.

"You did it, you did it," she crooned. To Lee, who was dancing at the edge of the course, she yelled, "Hooray, he did the teeter-totter by himself! Now all that leaves is the sway bridge. He's pretty good on the dog walk already; it's just the stuff that moves under him that panics him. Oh whoopee, I didn't think he was ever going to get that teeter-totter."

They finished the course, skipping the sway bridge but navigating everything else in good style and finishing fast down the flight of jumps. Cory dropped to the grass where Lee was sitting and puffed for breath.

"Did you bring the stopwatch?" she asked.

Lee nodded. "I'm ready any time you are."

"Okay, but let's take a breather first. I want him at his best the first time we time him."

"How long has he got to run the course?" Lee asked.

"Well, I'm going to say forty-eight seconds. According to the book they set different course times for different shows. It depends on how many yards long the actual travel distance is around the course, and how difficult the obstacles are. But that show up in Minnesota used forty-eight seconds as their running time, so I'd guess that's about average. Then if you go over the time limit you get one penalty point for every second of overtime.

"See, a perfect score is two hundred points, and a passing score is a hundred seventy. But you can lose points going around the course, like if you miss one of the weave poles or break from the pause box before the five-second limit. So say you make a perfect round, you'd have thirty seconds' worth of penalty time before you flunked. I know Sterling isn't going to win at this sport; that would be totally unrealistic. . . ."

"So what's your goal?"

"Our goal," Cory said firmly, "is a passing score. Just a passing score, to prove that we did it."

She stood up abruptly, unable to wait any longer to find out how close they were to their dream. "Okay now, we'll get lined up by the starting rocks; you call ready, set, go, and time us till Sterling crosses the finish line. Same as the starting line. We'll skip the sway bridge for now. Okay? All set?"

Girl and dog stood tensely at the starting line, her hand on his collar, her legs bent in sprinter style.

"Okay, this is it," Lee called. "Ready . . . set . . . GO!"

Sterling moved forward at a controlled canter. Over the first jump in a good straight line, and the second. By the third jump he was veering slightly to the left. "In," Cory said, and he corrected, coming over the jump at an awkward angle, too sharply approaching Cory's voice. She kept a steady line of sound for him, words, a monotone hum, anything to guide him.

The fourth jump he sailed over crookedly but successfully. Cory swung in close beside him and guided him with a quick "Over—SIT" into the pause box. She counted five, urged him out, and, walking close beside him, aligned him with the end of the teeter-totter. "Up easy," she urged, and up he went. He paused on the balance point, came down with the board, and trotted victoriously onward.

No time for a hug now. "Fast UP," she yelled, and he broke into a canter, leaping on the word *UP* and hitting the scaling wall well up. He scrambled over, skittered down the other side, and joined Cory for the run past the sway bridge. They were back near the starting line now. Lee had set into place the two weave poles that had been moved aside for the starting run.

"Out, in. Out, in." Sterling danced through the line of poles perfectly. He could smell them close beside his face and maneuvered between them smoothly, proudly. Then into the long curved tunnel, again finding his way by the closeness of the fabric scents on either side of him.

Cory met him at the end of the tunnel and guided him onto the ramp leading up the dog walk. Carefully he walked its length and slid down the far ramp. Then into the closed tunnel, burrowing under its flap, through the weave hoops. "In," Cory called, and Sterling veered right. The flight of jumps lay ahead of him. Joyful now, he picked up speed.

"Over, over, over, over." He flew over the jumps and ran toward Cory's voice, knowing the course was finished, high with the thrill of its completion.

The stopwatch clicked. Cory leaned close to Lee to read it. "Oh," she said, deflated. "Ninety-eight seconds. I thought he was going really well. Darn. I didn't think he was going slow at all. That's way beyond passing time, nowhere near perfect time, and we didn't even do the sway bridge." Sighing, she sank to the grass.

Squinting into the sunset, Lee said, "His speed will improve. You've got time."

"Not enough, not for the Saint Paul show." Cory's depression was rooted in the fear that no amount of time would be enough, that Sterling would never be able to get around the course fast enough for a passing score.

"So what are you going to do about entering him at Saint Paul?" Lee asked. "My folks are going, and you can go with us if you think he'll be ready, but entries close next Wednesday."

"That show is three weeks away," Cory said. "He's not going to be ready by then. I know he's not. He'll have to be a lot more confident on the obstacles before I can hope to get his speed up where it needs to be. I don't even know if he'll be doing the sway bridge by that time."

"So when would the next show that has Agility be?" Lee asked.

"Not till next spring, that same one we went to in April, at Mankato. I've got the whole list of shows from the Agility club, and there aren't any more in this part of the country till Mankato next April."

"Well? That's okay, isn't it? You've got no time limit on this, Cor. Hardly anybody even knows you're doing it. You're trying to prove something here, and if you ask me you've already proved it. Just getting a blind dog around an obstacle course like this, that's really an accomplishment."

"I know, but . . ."

"You want all that glory, doing it in public at a show." Lee grinned, and Cory grinned back.

"I have to do it all the way. I was aiming for the Saint Paul show, but if that's not realistic, I'll just set back my schedule and aim for Mankato in the spring."

Lee nodded.

"That'll give me more time," Cory went on, "to make sure he'll work in a strange place. I'll have to get Mom or Daddy or somebody to help me move the course to some different locations this fall, to a park or somewhere, so Sterling can get used to following my commands even in strange places with distracting noises. This place has been perfect, but . . ."

She looked around the oval. It had become dear to her over the summer. The very air seemed impregnated with her labor behind the lawn mower, her jubilation over Sterling's conquest of obstacle after obstacle, her gritty patience in the face of his fears.

There had been the nights when Lee came down the woodsy path to help and to cheer, and the nights when Mom had walked down to watch, when Iva or Dad and Diana had come. Their interest was good and warming, and it lay in the deepening blue night air of this clearing.

At Lee's touch on her shoulder, Cory stood and moved toward the wrought-iron gate, Sterling close beside her leg. She stopped for a moment to look back and smile.

It was night still, but Sterling woke instantly, alert to the girl's despair. Her arms pulled him tight against her chest and held him there. Softly he whined and struggled to lick the salt from her eyes and cheeks.

Her darkness of spirit crept into him like a black fog and alerted the deepest of his instincts. Some terrible sadness was coming. He felt this, and he pressed closer to her, to comfort and be comforted.

Ten

Sleeping and waking blended; Cory found her face wet with tears before she was fully aware of the dream or of the waking. The dream itself had already faded beyond her reach; it left only an imprint of malaise, a feeling that their time together, hers and Sterling's, was coming to an end.

Whether it was the dream or her deep thoughts, Cory wasn't sure, but the feeling flooded through her with the strength of fact.

If I don't go today, she thought, would that put it off? If I just say I don't want to go to Mankato, that I don't think Sterling's ready yet, would that mean I could keep him forever?

But it was all nonsense. Her mind cleared now. She'd had a dream because today was Sterling's day to prove himself in public and she was scared about that. Dreams came from what you were thinking about, consciously or subconsciously, so all that dream was, really, was her subconscious fear that once Sterling had run in the Agility test, somehow that would mean they'd accomplished what Fate, or whatever, intended them to accomplish for each other, and somehow or other he'd disappear from her life. It was all silly and stupid and it didn't mean a thing.

She rolled over to look at her alarm clock. Four-thirty. Almost time. She turned off the alarm and rose to meet the day.

They drove through the early-morning light, across northern Iowa, Nan and Iva in the front seat of Nan's little car, Cory and Sterling in the back. Lee had gone the day before with her parents in the motor home for Saturday's show and would meet Cory at the Mankato show grounds. Nan and Iva chatted like old friends; Cory and Sterling rode silent.

The Agility test, which was included in the show's premium list as "for exhibition only," was scheduled for two o'clock in the afternoon. Although Cory had followed their progress across Iowa and up into Minnesota on the road maps and despaired of their arriving on time, the little blue car pulled into the campus parking lot beside the show building at just after noon.

Nan and Iva left to look around. Cory took a folding chair from the trunk and led Sterling to the west side of the building, where the Agility course was to be set up. There they waited while the minutes on Cory's watch moved past with unbelievable slowness.

The dog sat beside her chair, pressing his body against her leg. Cory stroked his head. He was as ready as she could make him; that thought was her comfort now. His runs on the training course were down to between fifty and sixty seconds usually. On several weekends Ron and Diana had loaded the course in their Bronco and moved it to a park for practice runs—not the whole course, not the bigger, bulkier obstacles, but the jumps and the weave poles and the small tunnel. At first Sterling had been confused and hesitant, but after a few sessions he learned to listen only to Cory's voice, and to follow it as he did at home.

The home course had been altered and varied, too, so that he couldn't rely on memory to find his way through but was forced to follow Cory's word commands. There might be three jumps or five; the pause box, the dog walk, and the tunnel might be here or there or anywhere.

Around noon Dad and Diana appeared. They hadn't said for sure that they were coming. Ron had hedged, saying he might have an open house that day, but the gleam in Diana's eye had reassured Cory. Still, she was relieved when they came across the grass toward her, carrying between them a cooler and a pair of lawn chairs.

"I brought sandwiches," Diana said. "You want one?"

"Are you kidding?" Cory's stomach rolled at the thought.

At one-thirty a flatbed truck backed onto the lawn and men began lifting down equipment, rings and boards and gate-folded show-ring fencing. Cory sat forward, keen to see what the layout would be. Other dogs were gathering now, the corgi that Cory remembered from last year, a dozen shelties, and as many dogs of other breeds.

"You're here," a man's voice said above her. Startled, Cory looked up. It was the judge from last year.

"Hi."

"Are you showing him this year?" the man asked. "This is the blind dog, isn't it? I remember talking to you here last spring. I wondered if you were working with him on it."

"Yes." Cory glowed. "We've been working all year. I built a training course. He does pretty good, I think. Are you going to be judging again this year?"

He nodded. "There aren't very many qualified judges yet in this sport. Well, good luck. We'll all be pulling for you." He walked away and stopped to talk to several other people, all of whom looked toward Cory and smiled or gave her a thumbs-up sign.

Nan and Iva, Ron and Diana, Lee and her parents all gathered close to the ring as Cory and Sterling joined the knot of exhibitors at the entrance end of the course. "Good luck," "Hang tough," "Go get 'em,"—their cheers sent her into battle.

The dogs were divided into three classes, mini, midi, and maxi, according to their size. The small dogs ran first. In the class were two Yorkies, a West Highland white terrier, three cairn terriers, and a miniature dachshund. With the jumps set at eight inches, the little dogs dashed through the course one at a time. One cairn got so excited he ran straight out of the ring at the end of the line of jumps. His owner laughed along with the crowd as the dog was retrieved in dishonor. One Yorkie lay down and quit inside the closed tunnel rather than force her way under the cloth. The miniature dachshund ran a perfect course, except for the weave poles, which he ignored completely.

Scores were announced, winners awarded their ribbons.

Cory tensed.

"Midi class, line up for your run-through," the ring steward called, and Cory fell into line behind the starting marker. One by one the dogs and handlers moved out onto the course for their warm-up runs, to give the dogs a taste of the course.

Sterling moved jerkily, distracted by the closeness of the other dogs. Cory's heart sank. But he did negotiate the jumps and all of the obstacles, although she had to position him with her hands at the end of the teeter-totter.

The course was cleared; the first dog and handler took their positions on the starting line.

Cory clapped and cheered on each of the dogs who ran their courses before her turn, but in truth she was too nervous to enjoy their performances.

"Number Thirty-Four, Bedlington terrier," the steward called.

Cory slipped off Sterling's lead and guided him by the collar to the starting line. The judge met her eye and winked. "Good luck," he said, holding his stopwatch in his fist.

Sterling tensed. Cory braced herself, not daring to look toward her family.

"Ready . . . set . . . GO."

"Go Sterling, over . . . over . . . IN! Out!" He swerved between the second and third jumps, overcorrecting his line of travel at the shrillness of her voice. Cory fought down her panic and steadied her tone.

"Good boy, now over, now in, easy, good boy, over, sit!" Sterling sat quickly, hitting one edge of the pause box with his tail and shifting aside. The count of five came from the judge, and on they flew. "Easy UP." Onto the teeter-totter. "Steady." He balanced and rode it down.

Onto the sway bridge. Sterling froze in the middle, crouching and gripping the slats of wood with his toenails.

"Good boy, that's it. Keep going. Good! Now steady, out, in, out, in . . ."

He worked his way flawlessly through the line of weave poles. Into the tunnel he trotted, head up, sniffing and listening for guidance. He was moving at a good, steady clip, but nothing like the whiz-bang speed of the shelties who had gone before him. Cory prayed and tried not to think of the seconds ticking away.

Sterling came at the dog-walk ramp from an awkward angle. Swiftly Cory stepped close, moved him in a circle, and headed him at it again. Up onto the plywood ramp he stepped, and trotted across like a circus tightrope walker, bounding down on the far side. He gathered speed through the weave hoops and dove with genuine relish through the closed tunnel, making a moving blue-denim hump of himself, emerging joyously at the end.

Just the jumps left. "In, in, good boy, now go! Over, over, over, over!"

Fighting tears of happiness, Cory raced after Sterling across the finish line and into her mother's arms.

Five of the thirteen dogs in the midi Agility class were called back into the ring as achievers of passing scores. Three were shelties, one was a schnauzer, and one was a woolly silver dog who kept his face pressed against his owner's leg throughout the presentation.

The judge turned toward the audience and raised his voice to announce: "First place in the midi division goes to Number Thirty-Nine, sheltie, with a clear round and a running time of thirty-eight seconds."

Cory clapped with abandon. She knew the other winners had faster times than Sterling's. It didn't matter. He had passed, that was all. Her mother was grinning at her from ringside and nudging strangers to point out her daughter. Lee was punching the sky with a victorious fist and grinning, and even Todd and Trish Winterbottom looked pleased.

Cory's glance moved on, swiftly. Ron and Diana and Iva were lurching against each other in a three-sided dance hug, Diana's face twisted in self-defense away from Iva's cigarette.

The judge's voice went on, gaining volume now.

"Fourth place, with a clean round and a running time of fifty-one seconds, is a dog that just did something incredible. You folks don't know it, but this Bedlington terrier here, who just did a clean round with a very good running time, is completely blind. This young lady has worked very hard to bring her dog along, and I think they both deserve a big hand."

The judge handed Cory her white ribbon for fourth place, then with a spontaneous swoop he hugged her. The laughter and applause sent her heart soaring.

The pain was absolute and overwhelming. Sterling lay on the stainless-steel table, listening to the voices passing above him. The girl's snuffling sounds were what he tried to focus on. But the pain in his gut roared through him, making his ears ring. He slid away from the pain in a dark descent to a place where it didn't hurt, where nothing hurt anymore.

Afterword

Copper toxicosis. The words burned through Cory. For four days now Sterling had been very sick, and the words filled her mind. Copper toxicosis.

He had begun losing weight in late April, not long after the triumph at Mankato. The veterinarian had done what he called an SGPT test, then a surgical liver biopsy that had shown alarming amounts of copper in the liver tissue.

"It's like Wilson's disease in humans," the veterinarian had explained, as though by talking it through he could lessen the blow. "It's inherited and it's in several breeds of dogs, but it's worst in Bedlington terriers. If you catch it in time the dogs can sometimes be kept alive on medication, but not when it's this far advanced. The liver doesn't do its job, you see. It's supposed to flush excess copper from the dog's system and when it doesn't, then the copper builds up and causes liver damage and eventual death. I'm so sorry."

All last night Cory had cradled Sterling in her arms and cried into his woolly coat. His pain had been severe, and now he was close to death. Nan took the day off from work and Cory from school, and together they made the saddest of trips to the pet hospital at the edge of town.

The doctor looked now at Cory, the question in his eyes. She nodded.

"Do you want to wait outside?" he asked her.

"No, he needs me with him."

The man nodded and the injection was delivered.

Corianne's grief went beyond missing her beloved dog. The emptiness in Cory was for herself as well — she missed the importance Sterling gave her. She missed, dreadfully, the knowledge that to one living being she was all-important.

This then, she told herself one day, this was what had held her mother in despair for so long after Bethy's death. Not lack of love for Cory, but grief for the loss of the little girl to whom Nan had been the world.

It was gently healing knowledge.

On a summer night, the first day of vacation, Cory walked down the woodsy path to lean her arms on the wrought-iron gate.

Beyond the rim of trees stood the white plastic pipe

hurdles, the faded denim tunnels, and the warping planks of teeter-totter and dog walk. It was time to move them. Past time. The lawn-care company needed access to the lower garden. Already the grass was up to the bottom bars on the jumps, and weeds were twice as high. Time to store the stuff in the garage until she could think of what to do with it.

Suddenly Cory lifted her head and stared. In the blue haze of summer twilight, a flash of white appeared on the course.

It was Sterling.

He sailed down the flight of jumps toward her, finding her with perfect eyes, his long pink tongue lolling from the side of his mouth.

He galloped toward her, then spun away playfully and tore around the edge of the clearing. He leaped onto the teeter-totter and stayed on as it crashed down. He flung himself onto the scaling wall, rocking it. The sway bridge moved and dipped beneath his feet.

Cory stared, transfixed.

Again he whirled and sailed the flight of jumps, away from her this time, to fade into the far shadows.